PUBLIC LIBRARY

San Anselmo, California

●

This book is due on the last day stamped below.
A fine of Five Cents will be charged for each day the
book is kept after the date stamped.

Rose Fairy Book

ROSE
FAIRY
BOOK

COLLECTED AND EDITED BY

Andrew Lang

ILLUSTRATED BY

Vera Bock

WITH A FOREWORD BY

Mary Gould Davis

DAVID McKAY COMPANY, INC.

NEW YORK

'Father Grumbler,' 'The Knights of the Fish,' from *The Brown Fairy Book*, c 1904, renewed
1931; 'Donkey Skin,' 'The Queen of the Flowery Isles,' 'What Came of Picking Flowers,'
'Fortunatus and His Purse,' 'The Story of Bensurdatu,' 'The Bear,' 'Bobino,' from *The
Grey Fairy Book*, c 1900, renewed 1928; 'A Lost Paradise,' 'The False Prince and the True,'
'The Castle of Kerglas,' from *The Lilac Fairy Book*, c 1910, renewed 1937; 'The Frog and
the Lion Fairy,' 'The White Doe,' from *The Orange Fairy Book*, c 1906, renewed 1933;
'The Seven Who Helped,' formerly 'How the Hermit Helped To Win the King's Daughter,'
'The Sprig of Rosemary,' 'The Golden Lion,' 'The Water of Life,' from *The Pink Fairy
Book*, c 1897, renewed 1924.

FIRST EDITION JUNE 1948
REPRINTED MAY 1949
NOVEMBER 1951
AUGUST 1954
MARCH 1966
DECEMBER 1967

Printed in the United States of America
VAN REES PRESS • NEW YORK

Foreword

FROM the *Grey*, the *Brown*, the *Pink*, the *Lilac* and the *Orange Fairy Books* the editors have selected this group of romantic tales that have their origin in the Latin languages—French, Italian and Spanish.

Some of them are familiar, some less well known; but they all have the atmosphere of Fairyland. Andrew Lang had a rather special feeling for the folk tales in which a brave and resourceful hero, aided by the "over the border" people, rescued and married the lovely heroine. These old tales are, he felt, the foundation of what he calls the literary fairy tale, like his own *Prince Prigio* and Thackeray's *The Rose and the Ring*. He cites Charles Perrault's *Contes de ma Mére Oie*, published in 1697, as "laying the foundation of the fairy edifice." Of Madame d'Aulnoy, who followed Perrault, he says, "Madame d'Aulnoy is the true mother of the modern fairy tale. She invented the modern Court of Fairyland, with its manners, its fairies, its queens, its amorous, its cruel, its good, its evil, its odious, its friendly fées." "The White Cat," the most famous of Madame d'Aulnoy's stories and one of the most charming of all French fairy tales, Andrew Lang put into the *Blue Fairy Book* along with Perrault's "Cinderella," "Little Red Riding Hood," "The Sleeping Beauty" and "Puss-in-Boots."

There are two of Madame d'Aulnoy's stories in this volume. Here, too, are tales from Sicily that are variants of the romantic fairy stories of southern Spain. Many of the themes here can be traced to the famous Italian collection called *Lo Cunto de li Cunti* or *Il Pentamerone*. It was written in the seventeenth century by Giambattista Basile in a Neapolitan dialect that later went out of use. The stories were buried until, in the late nineteenth century, the Italian poet and philosopher, Benedetto Croce, and his students translated them into modern Italian. Soon afterward Professor Penzer translated them into English with highly important notes and annotations. In this book one can trace the basic theme of most of the fairy tales of the Western Hemisphere, from "East of the Sun and West of the Moon" to "The Golden Lion," which is in Spain called "The Golden Parrot."

There is not as much humor in these stories as there is in the folk tales of the Slavic people or those of the Scandinavian countries. But there is a certain dignity and graciousness, an emphasis on the good in its conflict with the evil that appeals to boys and girls, just as it appealed to the great editor who searched for and found the tales and had them translated into English. Andrew Lang had a deep faith in childhood. "I have often thought," he said, "that most children have a touch of genius which fades into the light of common day as they reach the age of eight or nine."

Andrew Lang was born more than one hundred years ago, on March 31, 1844, in the little town of Selkirk in Scotland. "It was worth while then," he says, "to be a boy in the south of Scotland, and to fish the waters haunted by old legends, musical with old songs." He speaks of "the long, lounging, solitary days beneath the woods of Ashiestiel—days so lovely that they sometimes in the end begat a superstitious eeriness; one seemed forsaken in an enchanted world; one might see the two white fairy deer flit by, bringing to us, as to Thomas the Rhymer, the tidings that we must back to Fairyland."

In our sorry world of today boys and girls will be all the better for a trip with Andrew Lang to his Fairyland.

MARY GOULD DAVIS

January, 1948

Contents

Illustrations

Donkey Skin

T

HERE WAS ONCE UPON
a time a king who was so much beloved by his subjects that
he thought himself the happiest monarch in the whole world,
and he had everything his heart could desire. His palace was
filled with the rarest of curiosities and his gardens with the
sweetest flowers, while in the marble stalls of his stables stood
a row of milk-white Arabs, with big brown eyes.

Strangers who had heard of the marvels which the king had
collected, and made long journeys to see them, were, however,
surprised to find the most splendid stall of all occupied by a
donkey, with particularly large and drooping ears. It was a
very fine donkey, but still, as far as they could tell, nothing so
very remarkable as to account for the care with which it was
lodged. They went away wondering, for they could not know
that every night, when it was asleep, bushels of gold pieces
tumbled out of its ears, which were picked up each morning by
the attendants.

After many years of prosperity a sudden blow fell upon the
king in the death of his wife, whom he loved dearly. But before
she died, the queen, who had always thought first of his happiness, gathered all her strength and said to him:

'Promise me one thing: you must marry again, I know, for the good of your people, as well as of yourself. But do not set about it in a hurry. Wait until you have found a woman more beautiful and better formed than myself.'

'Oh, do not speak to me of marrying,' sobbed the king, 'rather let me die with you.' But the queen only smiled faintly, turned over on her pillow and died.

For some months the king's grief was great; then gradually he began to forget a little, and, besides, his counsellors were always urging him to seek another wife. At first he refused to listen to them, but by-and-by he allowed himself to be persuaded to think of it, only stipulating that the bride should be more beautiful and attractive than the late queen, according to the promise he had made her.

Overjoyed at having obtained what they wanted, the counsellors sent envoys far and wide to get portraits of all the most famous beauties of every country. The artists were very busy and did their best, but alas! Nobody could even pretend that any of the ladies could compare for a moment with the late queen.

At length, one day, when he had turned away discouraged from a fresh collection of pictures, the king's eyes fell on his adopted daughter, who had lived in the palace since she was a baby, and he saw that, if a woman existed on the whole earth more lovely than the queen, this was she! He at once made known what his wishes were, but the young girl, who was not at all ambitious and had not the faintest desire to marry him, was filled with dismay and begged for time to think about it. That night, when everyone was asleep, she started in a little car drawn by a big sheep and went to consult her fairy godmother.

'I know what you have come to tell me,' said the fairy, when the maiden stepped out of the car, 'and if you don't wish to marry him, I will show you how to avoid it. Ask him to give you a dress that exactly matches the sky. It will be impossible for him to get one, so you will be quite safe.'

The girl thanked the fairy and returned home again.

The next morning, when her father—as she had always called him—came to see her, she told him that she could give him no answer until he had presented her with a dress the color of the sky.

The king, overjoyed at this answer, sent for all the choicest weavers and dressmakers in the kingdom and commanded them to make a robe the color of the sky without an instant's delay, or he would cut off their heads at once.

Dreadfully frightened at this threat, they all began to dye and cut and sew, and in two days they brought back the dress, which looked as if it had been cut straight out of the heavens!

The poor girl was thunderstruck, and did not know what to do; so in the night she harnessed her sheep again and went in search of her godmother.

'The king is cleverer than I thought,' said the fairy, 'but tell him you must have a dress of moonbeams.'

And the next day, when the king summoned her into his presence, the girl told him what she wanted.

'Madam, I can refuse you nothing,' said he. And he ordered the dress to be ready in twenty-four hours or every man should be hanged.

They set to work with all their might, and by dawn next day the dress of moonbeams was laid across her bed. The girl, though she could not help admiring its beauty, began to cry till the fairy, who heard her, came to her help.

'Well, I could not have believed it of him!' said she. 'But ask for a dress of sunshine and I shall be surprised indeed if he manages that!'

The goddaughter did not feel much faith in the fairy after her two previous failures but, not knowing what else to do, she told her father what she was bidden.

The king made no difficulties about it and even gave his finest rubies and diamonds to ornament the dress, which was so dazzling, when finished, that it could not be looked at save through smoked glasses!

When the princess saw it, she pretended that the sight hurt her eyes and retired to her room, where she found the fairy awaiting her, very much ashamed of herself.

'There is only one thing to be done now!' cried she. 'You must demand the skin of the donkey he sets such store by. It is from that donkey he obtains all his vast riches, and I am sure he will never give it to you.'

The princess was not so certain. However, she went to the king and told him she could never marry him till he had given her the donkey's skin.

The king was both astonished and grieved at this new request, but did not hesitate an instant. The donkey was sacrificed, and the skin laid at the feet of the princess.

The poor girl, seeing no escape from the fate she dreaded, wept afresh, and tore her hair; when, suddenly, the fairy stood before her.

'Take heart,' she said, 'all will now go well! Wrap yourself in this skin, leave the palace and go as far as you can. I will look after you. Your dresses and your jewels shall follow you underground, and if you strike the earth whenever you need anything, you will have it at once. But go quickly; you have no time to lose.'

So the princess clothed herself in the donkey's skin and slipped from the palace without being seen by anyone.

Directly she was missed there was a great hue and cry, and every corner, possible and impossible, was searched. Then the king sent out parties along all the roads, but the fairy threw her invisible mantle over the girl when they approached and none of them could see her.

The princess walked on a long, long way, trying to find someone who would take her in and let her work for them. But though the cottagers, whose houses she passed, gave her food from charity, the donkey skin was so dirty they would not allow her to enter their houses. For her flight had been so hurried there had been no time to clean it.

Tired and disheartened at her ill-fortune she was wandering, one day, past the gate of a farmyard situated just outside the walls of a large town, when she heard a voice calling to her. She turned and saw the farmer's wife standing among her turkeys and making signs to her to come in.

'I want a girl to wash the dishes and feed the turkeys, and clean out the pig sty,' said the woman, 'and, to judge by your dirty clothes, you would not be too fine for the work.'

The girl accepted her offer with joy, and she was at once set to work in a corner of the kitchen, where all the farm servants came and made fun of her and the donkey skin in which she was wrapped. But by-and-by they were so used to the sight of it that it ceased to amuse them, and the girl worked so hard and so well that her mistress grew quite fond of her. And she was so clever at keeping sheep and herding turkeys that you would have thought she had done nothing else during her whole life!

One day she was sitting on the banks of a stream, bewailing her wretched lot, when she suddenly caught sight of herself in the water. Her hair and part of her face was quite concealed by the ass's head, which was drawn right over like a hood, and the dirty matted skin covered her whole body. It was the first time she had seen herself as other people saw her and she was filled with shame at the spectacle. Then she threw off her disguise and jumped into the water, plunging in again and again, till she shone like ivory.

When it was time to go back to the farm she was forced to put on the skin which disguised her and now seemed more dirty than ever; but, as she did so, she comforted herself with the thought that tomorrow was a holiday and she would be able for a few hours to forget that she was a farm girl and be a princess once more.

So, at break of day, she stamped on the ground, as the fairy had told her, and instantly the dress like the sky lay across her tiny bed. Her room was so small there was no place for the train of her dress to spread itself out, but she pinned it up carefully when she combed her beautiful hair and piled it high on top of her head as she had always worn it. Then she was so pleased with herself that she determined never to let a chance pass of putting on her splendid clothes, even if she had to wear them in the fields, with no one to admire her but the sheep and turkeys.

Now the farm was a royal farm and, one holiday, when 'Donkey Skin'—as they had nicknamed the princess—had locked the door of her room and clothed herself in her dress of sunshine, the king's son rode through the gate and asked if he might come and rest himself a little after hunting. Some food and milk were set before him in the garden, and when he felt rested he began to explore the house, which was famous throughout the whole kingdom for its age and beauty.

He opened one door after the other, admiring the old rooms,

when he came to a handle that would not turn. He stooped and peeped through the keyhole to see what was inside and was greatly astonished at beholding a beautiful girl, clad in a dress so dazzling that he could hardly look at it.

The dark gallery seemed darker than ever as he turned away, but he went back to the kitchen and inquired who slept in the room at the end of the passage. The scullery maid, they told him, whom everybody laughed at and called 'Donkey Skin.'

Though the prince perceived there was some strange mystery about this, he saw quite clearly there was nothing to be gained by asking any more questions. So he rode back to the palace, his head filled with the vision he had seen through the keyhole.

All night long he tossed about and awoke the next morning in a high fever. The queen, who had no other child and lived in a state of perpetual anxiety about this one, at once gave him up for lost, and indeed his sudden illness puzzled the greatest doctors, who tried the usual remedies in vain.

At last they told the queen that some secret sorrow must be at the bottom of all this, and she threw herself on her knees beside her son's bed and implored him to confide his trouble to her. If it was ambition to be king, his father would gladly resign the cares of the crown and suffer him to reign in his stead; or, if it was love, everything should be sacrificed to get for him the wife he desired, even if she were daughter of a king with whom the country was at war at present!

'Madam,' replied the prince, whose weakness would hardly allow him to speak, 'do not think me so unnatural as to wish to deprive my father of his crown. As long as he lives I shall remain the most faithful of his subjects! And as to the princesses you speak of, I have seen none that I should care for as a wife, though I would always obey your wishes, whatever it might cost me.'

'Ah, my son,' cried she, 'we will do anything in the world to save your life—and ours too, for if you die, we shall die also.'

'Well, then,' replied the prince, 'I will tell you the only thing that will cure me—a cake made by the hand of Donkey Skin.'

'Donkey Skin!' exclaimed the queen, who thought her son had gone mad. 'And who or what is that?'

'Madam,' answered one of the attendants present, who had been with the prince at the farm, 'Donkey Skin is, next to the wolf, the most disgusting creature on the face of the earth. She is a girl who wears a black, greasy skin and lives at your farmer's as henwife.'

'Never mind,' said the queen. 'My son seems to have eaten some of her pastry. It is the whim of a sick man, no doubt, but send at once and have her bake a cake.'

The attendant bowed and ordered a page to ride with the message.

Now it is by no means certain that Donkey Skin had not caught a glimpse of the prince, either when his eyes looked through the keyhole, or else from her little window which was over the road. But whether she had actually seen him or only heard him spoken of, directly she received the queen's command, she flung off the dirty skin, washed herself from head to foot, and put on a skirt and bodice of shining silver. Then, she took the richest cream, the finest flour and the freshest eggs on the farm, and locking herself into her room, set about making her cake.

As she was stirring the mixture in the saucepan a ring that she sometimes wore in secret slipped from her finger and fell into the dough. Perhaps Donkey Skin saw it, or perhaps she did not; but, anyway, she went on stirring, and soon the cake was ready to be put in the oven. When it was nice and brown

she took off her dress, put on her dirty skin, and gave the cake to the page, asking at the same time for news of the prince. But the page turned his head aside and would not even condescend to answer.

The page rode like the wind, and as soon as he arrived at the palace he snatched up a silver tray and hastened to present the cake to the prince. The sick man began to eat it so fast that the doctors thought he would choke; indeed, he very nearly did, for the ring was in one of the bits which he broke off, though he managed to extract it from his mouth without anyone seeing him.

The moment the prince was left alone he drew the ring from under his pillow and kissed it a thousand times. Then he set his mind to find how he was to see the owner—for even he did not dare to confess that he had only beheld Donkey Skin through a keyhole, lest they should laugh at this sudden passion.

All this worry brought back the fever, which the arrival of the cake had diminished for the time, and the doctors, not knowing what else to say, informed the queen that her son was simply dying of love.

The queen, stricken with horror, rushed into the king's presence with the news, and together they hastened to their son's bedside.

'My boy, my dear boy,' cried the king, 'who is it you want to marry? We will give her to you for a bride even if she is the humblest of our slaves. What is there in the whole world that we would not do for you?'

The prince, moved to tears at these words, drew the ring, which was an emerald of the purest water, from under his pillow.

'Ah, dear father and mother, let this be a proof that the one I love is no peasant girl. The finger which that ring fits has never been thickened by hard work. But be her condition what it may, I will marry no other.'

The king and queen examined the tiny ring very closely, and agreed with their son that the wearer could be no mere farm girl. Then the king ordered heralds and trumpeters to go through the town, summoning every maiden to the palace. And she whom the ring fitted would some day be queen.

First came all the princesses, then all the duchesses' daughters, and so on, in proper order. But not one of them could slip the ring over the tip of her finger, to the great joy of the prince, whom excitement was fast curing. At last, when the high-born damsels had failed, the shopgirls and chambermaids took their turn, but with no better fortune.

'Call in the scullions and shepherdesses,' commanded the prince. But the sight of their red fingers satisfied everybody.

'There is not a woman left, Your Highness,' said the chamberlain. But the prince waved him aside.

'Have you sent for Donkey Skin, who made me the cake?' asked he. The courtiers began to laugh, and replied that they would not have dared to introduce so dirty a creature into the palace.

'Let someone go for her at once,' ordered the king. 'I commanded the presence of every maiden, high or low, and I meant it.'

The princess had heard the trumpets and the proclamations and knew quite well that her ring was at the bottom of it all. She, too, had fallen in love with the prince and many the dream she had had of him, and trembled with fear lest someone's finger might be as small as her own.

When, therefore, the messenger from the palace rode up to the gate, she was nearly beside herself with delight. Hoping all the time for such a summons she had dressed herself with great care, putting on the garment of moonlight, whose skirt was scattered over with emeralds. But when they began calling to her to come down, she hastily covered herself with her donkey skin and announced she was ready to present herself before his highness.

She was taken straight into the hall, where the prince was awaiting her, but at the sight of the donkey skin his heart sank. Had he been mistaken after all?

'Are you the girl,' he said, turning his eyes away as he spoke, 'are you the girl who has a room in the farthest corner of the inner court of the farmhouse?'

'Yes, my lord, I am,' answered she.

'Hold out your hand then,' continued the prince, feeling that he must keep his word, whatever the cost, and to the astonishment of every one present a little hand, white and delicate, came from beneath the black and dirty skin. The ring slipped on with the utmost ease and, as it did so, the skin fell to the ground, disclosing a figure of such beauty that the prince, weak as he was, fell on his knees before her, while the king and queen joined their prayers to his.

Indeed, their welcome was so warm and their caresses so bewildering that the princess hardly knew how to find words to reply, when the ceiling of the hall opened and the fairy godmother appeared seated in a car made entirely of white lilac. In a few words she explained the history of the princess and how she came to be there. Then, without losing a moment, preparations of the most magnificent kind were made for the wedding.

The kings of every country on the earth were invited, including, of course, the princess' adopted father, who by this time had married a widow, and not one refused.

But what a strange assembly it was! Each monarch traveled

in the way he thought most impressive. Some came borne in litters, others had carriages of every shape and kind, while the rest were mounted on elephants, tigers and even upon eagles.

So splendid a wedding had never been seen before; and when it was over the king announced that it was to be followed by a coronation, for he and the queen were tired of reigning and the young couple must take their place.

The rejoicings lasted for three whole months, then the new sovereigns settled down to govern their kingdom, and made themselves so much beloved by their subjects that when they died, a hundred years later, each man mourned them as his own father and mother.

[From *Le Cabinet des Fées.*]

The Queen of the Flowery Isles

HERE ONCE LIVED A queen who ruled over the Flowery Isles. To her extreme grief, her husband died a few years after their marriage. On being left a widow she devoted herself almost entirely to the education of the two charming princesses, her only children. The elder of them was so lovely that as she grew up her mother greatly feared she would excite the jealousy of the Queen of all the Isles, who prided herself on being the most beautiful woman in the world and insisted on all rivals bowing before her charms.

In order the better to gratify her vanity she had urged the king, her husband, to make war on all the surrounding islands. As his greatest wish was to please her, the only conditions he imposed on any newly conquered country was that each princess of every royal house should attend his court as soon as she was fifteen years old and do homage to the transcendent beauty of his queen.

The Queen of the Flowery Isles, well aware of this law, was fully determined to present her daughter to the proud queen as soon as her fifteenth birthday was past.

The Queen of all the Isles had heard a rumor of the young

princess' great beauty and awaited her visit with some anxiety. This soon developed into jealousy, for when the interview took place it was impossible not to be dazzled by such radiant charms, and the queen was obliged to admit she had never beheld anyone so exquisitely lovely.

Of course she thought, excepting myself, for nothing could have made her believe it possible that anyone could eclipse her. But the outspoken admiration of the entire court soon undeceived her and made her so angry that she pretended illness and retired to her own rooms, to avoid witnessing the princess' triumph.

She also sent word to the Queen of the Flowery Isles that she was sorry not to be well enough to see her again and advised her to return to her own land with the princess, her daughter. This message was entrusted to one of the great ladies of the court, who was an old friend of the Queen of the Flowery Isles, and who advised her not to wait to take a formal leave but to go home as fast as she could.

The queen was not slow to take the hint and lost no time in obeying it. Being well aware of the magic powers of the incensed queen, she warned her daughter that she was threatened by some great danger if she left the palace for any reason whatever during the next six months.

The princess promised obedience and no pains were spared to make the time pass pleasantly for her.

The six months were nearly at an end, and on the very last day a splendid fête was to take place in a lovely meadow quite near the palace. The princess, who had been able to watch all the preparations from her window, implored her mother to let her go as far as the meadow. The queen, thinking all risks must be over, consented and promised to take her there herself.

The whole court was delighted to see their much-loved princess at liberty, and everyone set off in high glee to join in the fête.

The princess, overjoyed at being once more in the open air, was walking a little in advance of her party when suddenly the earth opened under her feet and closed again after swallowing her up!

The queen fainted away with terror, and the young sister of the princess burst into floods of tears and could hardly be dragged away from the fatal spot, while the court was overwhelmed with horror at so great a calamity.

Orders were given to bore the earth to a great depth, but in vain. Not a trace of the vanished princess was to be found.

She sank right through the earth and found herself in a desert place, with nothing but rocks and trees and no sign of any human being. The only living creature she saw was a very pretty little dog that ran up to her and at once began to caress her. She took him in her arms and, after playing with him for a little, put him down again, when he started off in front of her, looking round from time to time as though begging her to follow.

She let him lead her on and presently reached a little hill, from which she saw a valley full of lovely fruit trees, bearing flowers and fruit together. The ground was also covered with fruit and flowers, and in the middle of the valley rose a fountain surrounded by a velvety lawn.

The princess hastened to this charming spot and, sitting down on the grass, began to think over the misfortune which had befallen her. She burst into tears as she reflected on her sad condition.

The fruit and clear fresh water would, she knew, prevent her from dying of hunger or thirst. But how could she escape if any wild beast appeared and tried to devour her?

At length, having thought over every possible evil which could happen, the princess tried to distract her mind by playing with the little dog. She spent the whole day near the fountain, but as night drew on she wondered what she should do, when she noticed the little dog was pulling at her dress.

She paid no heed to him at first, but as he continued to pull her dress and then run a few steps in one particular direction, she at last decided to follow him. He stopped before a rock with a large opening in the center, which he evidently wished her to enter.

The princess did so and discovered a large and beautiful cave lit up by the brilliancy of the stones with which it was lined, with a little couch covered with soft moss in one corner. She lay down on it and the dog at once nestled at her feet. Tired out with all she had gone through she soon fell asleep.

Next morning she was awakened very early by the songs of many birds. The little dog woke up too and sprang round her in his most caressing manner. The princess rose and went outside, the dog as before running on in front and turning back constantly to take her dress and draw her on.

She let him have his way and he soon led her back to the beautiful garden where she had spent part of the day before. Here she ate some fruit, drank some water of the fountain, and felt as if she had made an excellent meal. She walked about amongst the flowers, played with her little dog, and at night returned to sleep in the cave.

In this way the princess passed several months. As her first terrors died away she gradually became more resigned to her fate. The little dog was a great comfort and her constant companion.

One day she noticed that he seemed very sad and did not caress her as usual. Fearing he might be ill she carried him to a spot where she had seen him eat some particular herbs, hoping they might do him good, but he would not touch them. He spent all the night sighing and groaning as if in great pain.

At last the princess fell asleep. When she awoke her first thought was for her little pet, but not finding him at her feet as usual, she ran out of the cave to look for him. As she stepped out of the cave she caught sight of an old man, who hurried away so fast that she had hardly time to see him before he disappeared.

This was a fresh surprise and almost as great a shock as the loss of her little dog, who had been so faithful to her ever since the first day she had seen him. She wondered if he had strayed away or if the old man had taken him.

Tormented by all kinds of thoughts and fears she wandered on, when suddenly she felt herself wrapped in a thick cloud and carried through the air. She made no resistance and before very long found herself, to her great surprise, in an avenue leading to the palace in which she had been born. No sign of the cloud remained.

As the princess approached the palace she perceived that everyone was dressed in black, and she was filled with fear as to the cause of this mourning. She hastened on and was soon recognized and welcomed with shouts of joy. Her sister hearing the cheers ran out and embraced the wanderer, with tears of happiness, telling her that the shock of her disappearance had been so terrible their mother had only survived it a few days.

Since then the younger princess had worn the crown, which she now resigned to her sister to whom it by right belonged. But the elder wished to refuse it, and would only accept the crown on condition that her sister should share in all the power.

The first acts of the new queen were to do honor to the memory of her dear mother and to shower every mark of generous affection on her sister. Then, being still very grieved at the loss of her little dog, she had a careful search made for him in every country, and when nothing could be heard of him she offered half her kingdom to whoever should restore him to her.

Many gentlemen of the court, tempted by the thought of such a reward, set off in all directions in search of the dog. But all returned empty-handed to the queen who, in despair, announced that since life was unbearable without her little dog, she would give her hand in marriage to the man who brought him back.

The prospect of such a prize quickly turned the court into a desert, nearly every courtier starting on the quest. While they were away the queen was informed one day that a very ill-looking man wished to speak with her. She desired him to be shown into the room where she was sitting with her sister.

On entering her presence he said that he was prepared to give the queen her little dog if she on her side was ready to keep her word.

The princess was the first to speak. She said that the queen had no right to marry without the consent of the nation, and that on so important an occasion the general council must be summoned. The queen could not say anything against this statement, but she ordered an apartment in the palace to be given to the man and desired the council to meet on the following day.

Next day, accordingly, the council assembled in great state, and by the princess' advice it was decided to offer the man a large sum of money for the dog, and should he refuse it to banish him from the kingdom without seeing the queen again. The man refused the price offered and left the hall.

The princess informed the queen of what had passed, and the

queen approved of all but added that, as she was her own mistress, she had made up her mind to abdicate her throne and wander through the world till she had found her little dog.

The princess was much alarmed by such a resolution and implored the queen to change her mind. While they were discussing the subject, one of the chamberlains appeared to inform the queen that the bay was covered with ships. The two sisters ran to the balcony and saw a large fleet in full sail for the port.

In a little time they came to the conclusion that the ships must come from a friendly nation, as every vessel was decked with gay flags, streamers and pennons, and the way was led by a small ship flying a great white flag of peace.

The queen sent a special messenger to the harbor and was soon informed that the fleet belonged to the Prince of the Emerald Isles, who begged leave to land in her kingdom and present his humble respects to her. The queen at once sent some of the court dignitaries to receive the prince and bid him welcome.

She awaited him seated on her throne, but rose on his appearance and went a few steps to meet him. Then she begged him to be seated and for about an hour kept him in close conversation.

The prince was then conducted to a splendid suite of apartments. The next day he asked for a private audience and was admitted to the queen s own sitting room, where she was sitting alone with her sister.

After the first greetings the prince informed the queen that he had some very strange things to tell her, which she only would know to be true.

'Madam,' said he, 'I am a neighbor of the Queen of all the Isles; a small isthmus connects part of my states with hers. One day, when hunting a stag, I had the misfortune to meet her and, not recognizing her, I did not stop to salute her with all proper ceremony. You, Madam, know better than anyone how revengeful she is and that she is also a mistress of magic. I learned both facts to my cost.

'The ground opened under my feet, and I soon found myself in a far distant region transformed into a little dog, under which shape I had the honor to meet Your Majesty. After six months, the queen's vengeance not yet being satisfied, she further changed me into a hideous old man, and in this form I was so afraid of being unpleasant in your eyes, Madam, that I hid myself in the depths of the woods, where I spent three months more. At the end of that time I was so fortunate as to meet a benevolent fairy who delivered me from the proud queen's power and told me all your adventures and where to find you. I now come to offer you a heart which has been entirely yours, Madam, since first we met in the desert.'

A few days later a herald was sent throughout the kingdom to proclaim the joyful news of the marriage of the Queen of the Flowery Isles with the young prince. They lived happily for many years, and ruled their people well.

As for the bad queen, whose vanity and jealousy had caused so much mischief, the fairies took all her power away for a punishment.

[From *Le Cabinet des Fées*.]

What Came of Picking Flowers

THERE WAS ONCE A woman who had three daughters whom she loved very much. One day the eldest was walking in a water meadow when she saw a pink growing in the stream. She stooped to pick the flower, but her hand had scarcely touched it when she vanished altogether. The next morning the second sister went out into the meadow, to see if she could find any trace of the lost girl. As a branch of lovely roses lay trailing across her path, she bent down to move it away, and in so doing could not resist plucking one of the roses. In a moment she, too, had disappeared. Wondering what could have become of her two sisters, the youngest followed in their footsteps and fell a victim to a branch of delicious white jessamine. So the old woman was left without any daughters at all.

She wept and wept and wept, all day and all night, and went on weeping so long, that her son, who had been a little boy when his sisters disappeared, grew up to be a tall youth. Then one night he asked his mother to tell him what was the cause of her grief.

When he had heard the whole story, he said, 'Give me your

blessing, mother, and I will go and search the world till I find them.'

So he set forth, and after he had traveled several miles without any adventures, he came upon three big boys fighting in the road. He stopped and inquired what they were fighting about, and one of them answered:

'My lord, our father left to us, when he died, a pair of boots, a key and a cap. Whoever puts on the boots and wishes himself in any place will find himself there. The key will open every door in the world, and with the cap on your head no one can see you. Now our eldest brother wants to have all three things for himself, and we wish to draw lots for them.'

'Oh, that is easily settled,' said the youth. 'I will throw this stone as far as I can, and the one who picks it up first shall have the three things.'

So he took the stone and flung it, and while the three brothers were running after it, he hastily drew on the boots, and said, 'Boots, take me to the place where I shall find my eldest sister.'

The next moment the young man was standing on a steep mountain before the gates of a strong castle guarded by bolts and bars and iron chains. The key, which he had not forgotten to put in his pocket, opened the doors one by one, and he walked through a number of halls and corridors till he met a beautiful and richly dressed young lady who started back in surprise at the sight of him, and exclaimed:

'Oh, sir, how did you contrive to get in here?'

The young man replied that he was her brother and told her by what means he had been able to pass through the doors. In return, she told him how happy she was, except for one thing, and that was, her husband lay under a spell and could never break it till there should be put to death a man who could not die.

They talked together for a long time, and then the lady said he had better leave her as she expected her husband back at any moment, and he might not like a visitor to be there. But the young man assured her she need not be afraid, as he had with him a cap which would make him invisible.

They were still deep in conversation, when the door suddenly opened, and a bird flew in, but he saw nothing unusual, for at the first noise, the youth had put on his cap. The lady jumped up and brought a large golden basin, into which the bird flew, reappearing directly after as a handsome man.

Turning to his wife, he cried, 'I am sure someone is in the room!' She was frightened, and declared that she was quite alone, but her husband persisted, and in the end she had to confess the truth.

'But if he is really your brother, why did you hide him?' asked he. 'I believe you are not telling me the truth, and if he comes back I shall kill him!'

At this the youth took off his cap and came forward. Then the husband saw that he was indeed so like his wife that he doubted her word no longer and embraced his brother-in-law with delight.

Drawing a feather from his bird's skin, he said, 'If you are in danger and cry, "Come and help me, King of the Birds," everything will go well with you.'

The young man thanked him and went away, and after he had left the castle he told the boots they must take him to the place where his second sister was living. As before, he found himself at the gates of a huge castle, within which was his second sister, very happy with her husband, who loved her dearly, but longing for the moment when he should be set free from the spell that kept him half his life a fish.

When he came home and had been introduced by his wife to

her brother, he welcomed him warmly, and gave him a fish scale, saying, 'If you are in danger, call to me, "Come and help me, King of the Fishes," and everything will go well with you.'

The young man thanked him and took his leave, and when he was outside the gates he told the boots to take him to the place where his youngest sister lived. The boots carried him to a dark cavern, with steps of iron leading up to it.

Inside she sat, weeping and sobbing, and as she had done nothing else the whole time she had been there, the poor girl had grown very thin. When she saw a man standing before her, she sprang to her feet and exclaimed:

'Oh, whoever you are, save me and take me from this horrible place!'

Then he told her who he was, and how he had seen her sisters, whose happiness was spoilt by the spell under which both their husbands lay, and she, in turn, related her story.

She had been carried off in the water meadow by a horrible monster, who wanted to make her marry him and had kept her a prisoner all these years because she would not submit to his will. Every day he came to beg her to consent to his wishes, and to remind her that there was no hope of her being set free, as he was the most constant man in the world, and besides that he could never die.

At these words the youth remembered his two enchanted brothers-in-law; and he advised his sister to promise to marry the old man, if he would tell her why he could never die. Suddenly everything began to tremble, as if it was shaken by a whirlwind, and the old man entered, and flinging himself at the feet of the girl, he said:

'Are you still determined never to marry me? If so you will have to sit there weeping till the end of the world, for I shall always be faithful to my wish to marry you!'

'Well, I will marry you,' she said, 'if you will tell me why it is you can never die.'

Then the old man burst into peals of laughter. 'Ah, ah, ah! You are thinking how you would be able to kill me? Well, to do that, you would have to find an iron casket which lies at the bottom of the sea and has a white dove inside, and then you would have to find the egg which the dove laid, and bring it here, and dash it against my head.' And he laughed again in his certainty that no one had ever got down to the bottom of the sea, and that if he did, he never would find the casket or be able to open it.

When he could speak once more, he said, 'Now you will be obliged to marry me, as you know my secret.'

But she begged so hard that the wedding might be put off for three days that he consented and went away rejoicing at his victory.

When he had disappeared, the brother took off the cap, which had kept him invisible all this time, and told his sister not to lose heart as he hoped in three days she would be free. Then he drew on his boots and wished himself at the seashore, and there he was directly. Drawing out the fish scale, he cried:

'Come and help me, King of the Fishes!'

His brother-in-law swam up and asked what he could do. The young man related the story, and when he had finished, his listener summoned all the fishes to his presence. The last to arrive was a little sardine, who apologized for being so late, but said she had hurt herself by knocking her head against an iron casket that lay in the bottom of the sea.

The king ordered several of the largest and strongest of his subjects to take the little sardine as a guide and bring him the iron casket. They soon returned with the box placed across their backs and laid it down before him.

Then the youth produced the key, and said, 'Key, open that box!'

The key opened it, and though they were all crowding round, ready to catch it, the white dove within flew away.

It was useless to go after it, and for a moment the young man's heart sank. The next minute, however, he remembered that he still had his feather and drew it out, crying:

'Come to me, King of the Birds!'

A rushing noise was heard, and the King of the Birds perched on his shoulder and asked what he could do to help him. His brother-in-law told him the whole story, and when he had finished, the King of the Birds commanded all his subjects to hasten to his presence. In an instant the air was dark with birds of all sizes, and at the very last came the white dove, apologizing for being so late by saying that an old friend had arrived at her nest, and she had been obliged to give him some dinner.

The King of the Birds ordered some of them to show the young man the white dove's nest, and when they reached it, there lay the egg which was to break the spell and set them all free. When it was safely in his pocket, the young man told the boots to carry him straight to the cavern where his youngest sister sat awaiting him.

Now it was already far on into the third day, which the old man had fixed for the wedding, and when the youth reached the cavern with his cap on his head, he found the monster there, urging the girl to keep her word and let the marriage take place at once.

At a sign from her brother she sat down and invited the old monster to lay his head on her lap. He did so with delight, and her brother standing behind her back passed her the egg unseen. She took it, and dashed it straight at the horrible head,

and the monster started and, with a groan that people took for
the rumblings of an earthquake, turned over and died.

As the breath went out of his body the husbands of the two
eldest daughters resumed their proper shapes and, sending for
their mother-in-law, whose sorrow was so unexpectedly turned
into joy, they had a great feast, and the youngest sister was rich
to the end of her days with the treasures she found in the cave,
collected by the monster.

[From the Portuguese.]

Fortunatus and His Purse

ONCE UPON A TIME there lived in the city of Famagosta, in the island of Cyprus, a rich man called Theodorus. He ought to have been the happiest person in the whole world, as he had all he could wish for, and a wife and little son whom he loved dearly. But unluckily, after a short time, he always grew tired of everything and had to seek new pleasures. When people are made like this the end is generally the same, and before Fortunatus (for that was the boy's name) was ten years old, his father had spent all his money and had not a farthing left.

But though Theodorus had been so foolish he was not quite without sense, and set about getting work at once. His wife, instead of reproaching him, sent away the servants and sold their fine horses, and did all the work of the house herself, even washing the clothes of her husband and child.

Thus time passed till Fortunatus was sixteen. One day when they were sitting at supper, the boy said to Theodorus:

'Father, why do you look so sad? Tell me what is wrong and perhaps I can help you.'

'Ah, my son, I have reason enough to be sad. But for me you

would now have been enjoying every kind of pleasure, instead of being buried in this tiny house.'

'Oh, do not let that trouble you,' replied Fortunatus, 'it is time I made some money for myself. To be sure I have never been taught any trade. Still, there must be something I can do. I will go and walk on the seashore and think about it.'

Very soon—sooner than he expected—a chance came, and Fortunatus, like a wise boy, seized on it at once. The post offered him was that of page of the Earl of Flanders, and as the earl's daughter was just going to be married, splendid festivities were held in her honor, and at some of the tilting matches Fortunatus was lucky enough to win the prize. These prizes, together with presents from the lords and ladies of the court, who liked him for his pleasant ways, made Fortunatus feel quite a rich man.

But though his head was not turned by the notice taken of him, it excited the envy of some of the other pages about the court, and one of them, called Robert, invented a plot to move Fortunatus out of his way. So he told the young man that the earl had taken a dislike to him and meant to kill him. Fortunatus believed the story and, packing up his fine clothes and money, slipped away before dawn.

He went to a great many big towns and lived well, and as he was generous and not wiser than most youths of his age, he very soon found himself penniless. Like his father, he then began to think of work and tramped half over Brittany in search of it. Nobody seemed to want him, and he wandered about from one place to another, till he found himself in a dense wood, without any paths and not much light. Here he spent two whole days, with nothing to eat and very little water to drink, going first in one direction and then in another, but never being able to find his way out.

During the first night he slept soundly, too tired to fear either man or beast, but when darkness came on for the second time, and growls were heard in the distance, he grew frightened and looked about for a high tree out of reach of his enemies. Hardly had he settled himself comfortably in one of the forked branches, when a lion walked up to a spring that burst from a rock close to the tree and, crouching down, drank greedily. This was bad enough, but after all, lions do not climb trees, and as long as Fortunatus stayed up on his perch, he was quite safe.

But no sooner was the lion out of sight, than his place was taken by a bear, and bears, as Fortunatus knew very well, are tree climbers. His heart beat fast, and not without reason, for as the bear turned away he looked up and saw Fortunatus!

Now in those days every young man carried a sword slung to his belt, and it was a fashion that came in very handily for Fortunatus. He drew his sword, and when the bear had climbed within a yard of him, he made a fierce lunge forward. The bear, wild with pain, tried to spring, but the bough he was standing on broke with his weight, and he fell heavily to the ground.

Then Fortunatus descended from his tree—first taking good care to see no other wild animals were in sight—and killed him with a single blow. He was just thinking he would light a fire and make a hearty dinner off bear meat, which is not at all bad eating, when he beheld a beautiful lady standing by his side, leaning on a wheel, and her eyes hidden by a bandage.

'I am Dame Fortune,' she said, 'and I have a gift for you. Shall it be wisdom, strength, long life, riches, health or beauty? Think well, and tell me what you will have.'

But Fortunatus, who had proved the truth of the proverb that 'It's ill thinking on an empty stomach,' answered quickly,

'Good lady, let me have riches in such plenty that I may never again be as hungry as I am now.'

And the lady held out a purse and told him he had only to put his hand into it, and he and his children would always find ten pieces of gold. But when they were dead it would be a magic purse no longer.

At this news Fortunatus was beside himself with joy and could hardly find words to thank the lady. But she told him the best thing he could do was to find his way out of the wood and, before bidding him farewell, pointed out which path he should take.

He walked along it as fast as his weakness would let him, until a welcome light at a little distance showed him that a house was near. It turned out to be an inn, but before entering, Fortunatus thought he had better make sure of the truth of what the lady had told him and took out the purse and looked inside. Sure enough there were the ten pieces of gold, shining brightly.

Then Fortunatus walked boldly up to the inn and ordered them to get ready a good supper at once, for he was very hungry, and to bring him the best wine in the house. And he seemed to care so little what he spent that everybody thought he was a great lord and vied with each other who should run quickest when he called.

After a night passed in a soft bed, Fortunatus felt so much better that he asked the landlord if he could find him some men-servants and tell him where he could buy some good horses. The next thing was to provide himself with smart clothes, and then to take a big house where he could give great feasts to the nobles and beautiful ladies who lived in palaces round about.

In this manner a whole year soon slipped away, and Fortunatus was so busy amusing himself that he never once remembered his parents whom he had left behind in Cyprus. But though he was thoughtless, he was not bad-hearted. As soon as their existence crossed his mind, he set about making preparations to visit them, and as he did not like being alone he looked round for someone older and wiser than himself to travel with him.

It was not long before he had the good luck to come across an old man, who had left his wife and children in a far country, many years before, when he went out into the world to seek the fortune which he never found. He agreed to accompany Fortunatus back to Cyprus, but only on condition he should first be allowed to return for a few weeks to his own home before venturing to set sail for an island so strange and distant. Fortunatus agreed to his proposal and, as he was always fond of anything new, said that he would go with him.

The journey was long, and they had to cross many large rivers and climb over high mountains and find their way through thick woods, before they reached at length the old man's castle. His wife and children had almost given up hope of seeing him again and crowded eagerly round him. Indeed, it did not take Fortunatus five minutes to fall in love with the youngest daughter, the most beautiful creature in the whole world, whose name was Cassandra.

'Give her to me for my wife,' he said to the old man, 'and let us all go together to Famagosta.'

So a ship was bought, big enough to hold Fortunatus, the old man and his wife, and their five sons and five daughters. And the day before they sailed the wedding was celebrated with magnificent rejoicings, and everybody thought that Fortunatus must certainly be a prince in disguise.

But when they reached Cyprus, he learned to his sorrow that

both his father and mother were dead, and for some time he shut himself up in his house and would see nobody, full of shame at having forgotten them all these years. Then he begged that the old man and his wife would remain with him, and take the place of his parents.

For twelve years Fortunatus and Cassandra and their two little boys lived happily in Famagosta. They had a beautiful house and everything they could possibly want, and when Cassandra's sisters married the purse provided them each with a fortune. But at last Fortunatus grew tired of staying at home, and thought he should like to go out and see the world again.

Cassandra shed many tears at first when he told her of his wishes, and he had a great deal of trouble to persuade her to give her consent. But on his promising to return at the end of two years she agreed to let him go.

Before he went away he showed her three chests of gold, which stood in a room with an iron door and walls twelve feet thick. 'If anything should happen to me,' he said, 'and I should never come back, keep one of the chests for yourself and give the others to our two sons.'

Then he embraced them all and took ship for Alexandria.

The wind was fair and in a few days they entered the harbor, where Fortunatus was informed by a man, whom he met on landing, that if he wished to be well received in the town, he must begin by making a handsome present to the sultan.

'That is easily done,' said Fortunatus, and went into a goldsmith's shop where he bought a large gold cup which cost five thousand pounds. This gift so pleased the sultan that he ordered a hundred casks of spices to be given to Fortunatus, who put them on board his ship and commanded the captain to return to Cyprus and deliver them to his wife, Cassandra. Fortunatus next obtained an audience of the sultan and begged permission to travel through the country. This the sultan readily gave him, adding some letters to the rulers of other lands which Fortunatus might wish to visit.

Filled with delight at feeling himself free to roam through the world once more, Fortunatus set out on his journey without losing a day. From court to court he went, astonishing everyone by the magnificence of his dress and the splendor of his presents.

At length he grew as tired of wandering as he had been of staying at home, and returned to Alexandria, where he found the same ship that had brought him from Cyprus lying in the harbor. Of course the first thing he did was to pay his respects to the sultan, who was eager to hear about his adventures.

When Fortunatus had told them all, the sultan observed, 'Well, you have seen many wonderful things, but I have something to show you more wonderful still.' And he led him into a room where precious stone lay heaped against the walls.

Fortunatus' eyes were quite dazzled, but the sultan went on without pausing and opened a door at the farther end. As far as Fortunatus could see, the cupboard was quite bare, except for a little red cap, such as soldiers wear in Turkey.

'Look at this,' said the sultan.

'But there is nothing very valuable about it,' answered Fortunatus. 'I've seen a dozen better caps than that, this very day.'

'Ah,' said the sultan, 'you do not know what you are talking about. Whoever puts this cap on his head and wishes himself in any place, will find himself there in a moment.'

'But who made it?' asked Fortunatus.

'That I cannot tell you,' replied the sultan.

'Is it very heavy to wear?' asked Fortunatus.

'No, quite light,' replied the sultan, 'just feel it.'

Fortunatus took the cap and put it on his head, and then,

without thinking, wished himself back in the ship that was starting for Famagosta. In a second he was standing at the prow, while the anchor was being weighed, and while the sultan was repenting of his folly in allowing Fortunatus to try on the cap, the vessel was making fast for Cyprus.

When it arrived, Fortunatus found his wife and children well, but the two old people were dead and buried. His sons had grown tall and strong but, unlike their father, had no wish to see the world, and found their chief pleasure in hunting and tilting. In the main, Fortunatus was content to stay quietly at home, and if a restless fit did seize upon him, he was able to go away for a few hours without being missed, thanks to the cap, which he never sent back to the sultan.

By-and-by he grew old, and feeling that he had not many days to live, he sent for his two sons, and showing them the purse and cap, he said to them:

'Never part with these precious possessions. They are worth more than all the gold and lands I leave behind me. But never tell their secret, even to your wife or dearest friend. That purse has served me well for forty years, and no one knows whence I got my riches.'

Then he died and was buried by his wife Cassandra, and he was mourned in Famagosta for many years.

The Story of Bensurdatu

THERE WAS ONCE A
king and queen who had three wonderfully beautiful daughters, and their one thought, from morning till night, was how they could make the girls happy.

One day the princesses said to the king, 'Dear father, we want so much to have a picnic and eat our dinner in the country.'

'Very well, dear children, let us have a picnic by all means,' answered he, and gave orders that everything should be made ready.

When luncheon was prepared it was put into a cart, and the royal family stepped into a carriage and drove right away into the country. After a few miles they reached a house and garden belonging to the king, and close by was their favorite place for lunch. The drive had made them very hungry, and they ate with a hearty appetite till almost all the food had disappeared.

When they had quite done, they said to their parents, 'Now we should like to wander about the garden a little, but when you want to go home just call to us.'

And they ran off, laughing, down a green glade, which led to the garden. But no sooner had they stepped across the fence

44

than a dark cloud came down and covered them and prevented them seeing whither they were going.

Meanwhile the king and queen sat lazily among the heather, and an hour or two slipped away. The sun was dropping toward the horizon, and they began to think it was time to go home. So they called to their daughters, and called again, but no one answered them.

Frightened at the silence, they searched every corner of the garden, the house and the neighboring wood, but no trace of the girls was to be found anywhere. The earth seemed to have swallowed them up. The poor parents were in despair.

The queen wept all the way home, and for many days after, and the king issued a proclamation that whoever should bring back his lost daughters should have one of them to wife and should, after his death, reign in his stead.

Now two young knights were at that time living at the court, and when they heard the king's declaration, they said one to the other, 'Let us go in search of them; perhaps we shall be the lucky persons.'

And they set out, each mounted on a strong horse, taking with them a change of raiment and some money.

But though they inquired at every village they rode through, they could hear nothing of the princesses, and by-and-by their money was all spent, and they were forced to sell their horses or give up the search. Even this money only lasted a little while longer, and nothing but their clothes lay between them and starvation.

They sold the spare garments that were bound on their saddles, and went to the inn to beg for some food, as they were really starving. When, however, they had to pay for what they had eaten and drunk, they said to the host:

'We have no money, and naught but the clothes we stand

up in. Take these and give us instead some old rags, and let us stay here and serve you.'

And the innkeeper was content with the bargain, and the knights stayed and were his servants.

All this time the king and queen remained in their palace, hungering for their children, but not a word was heard either of them or of the young men who had gone to seek for them.

Now there was living in the palace a faithful servant of the king's called Bensurdatu, who had served him for many years, and when Bensurdatu saw how grieved the king was, he lifted up his voice and said to him:

'Your Majesty, let me go and seek your daughters.'

'No, no, Bensurdatu,' replied the king. 'Three daughters have I lost, and two knights, and shall I lose you also?'

But Bensurdatu said again, 'Let me now go, Your Majesty. Trust me, and I will bring you back your daughters.'

Then the king gave way and Bensurdatu set forth. He rode on till he came to the inn, where he dismounted and asked for food. It was brought by the two knights, whom he knew at once in spite of their miserable clothes. Much astonished, he asked them how in the world they came there.

They told him all their adventures, and he sent for the innkeeper, and said to him, 'Give them back their garments and I will pay everything they owe you.'

The innkeeper did as he was bade, and when the two knights were dressed in their proper clothes, they declared they would join Bensurdatu and with him seek for the king's daughters.

The three companions rode on for many miles, and at length they came to a wild place, without sign of a human being. It was growing dark and, fearing to be lost on this desolate spot, they pushed on their horses and, at last, saw a light in the window of a tiny hut.

'Who comes there?' asked a voice, as they knocked at the door.

'Oh, have pity on us, and give us a night's shelter,' replied Bensurdatu. 'We are three tired travelers who have lost our way.'

Then the door was opened by a very old woman, who stood back and beckoned them to enter. 'Whence do you come, and whither do you go?' asked she.

'Ah, good woman, we have a heavy task before us,' answered Bensurdatu, 'we are bound to carry the king's daughters back to the palace!'

'Oh, unhappy creatures,' cried she, 'you know not what you are doing! The king's daughters were covered by a thick cloud, and no one knows where they may now be.'

'Oh, tell us, if you know, my good woman,' entreated Bensurdatu, 'for with them lies all our happiness.'

'Even if I were to tell you,' answered she, 'you could not rescue them. To do that you would have to go to the very bottom of a deep river, and though certainly you would find the king's daughters there, yet the two eldest are guarded by two giants, while the youngest is watched by a serpent with seven heads.'

The two knights, who stood by listening, were filled with terror at her words and wished to return immediately; but Bensurdatu stood firm, and said:

'Now we have come so far we must carry the thing through. Tell us where the river is, good woman, so we may get there as soon as possible.'

And the old woman told them and gave them some cheese, wine and bread so they should not set forth starving. When they had eaten and drunk they laid themselves down to sleep.

The sun had only just risen above the hills next morning

before they all woke and, taking leave of the wise woman who had helped them, they rode on till they came to the river.

'I am the eldest,' said one of the knights, 'and it is my right to go down first.'

So the others fastened a cord round him, gave him a little bell, and let him down into the water. But scarcely had the river closed above his head when such dreadful rushing sounds and peals of thunder came crashing round about him that he lost all his courage, and rang his bell, if perchance it might be heard amidst all this clamor. Great was his relief when the rope began slowly to pull him upward.

Then the other knight plunged in, but he fared no better than the first and was soon on dry ground again.

'Well, you are a brave pair!' said Bensurdatu, as he tied the rope round his own waist. 'Let us see what will happen to me.' And when he heard the thunder and clamor round about him he said to himself, 'Oh, make as much noise as you like, it won't hurt me!'

When his feet touched the bottom he found himself in a large, brilliantly lighted hall. In the middle sat the eldest princess, and in front of her lay a huge giant, fast asleep. Directly she saw Bensurdatu she nodded to him and asked with her eyes how he had come there.

For answer he drew his sword, and was about to cut off the giant's head, when she stopped him quickly and made signs to hide himself, as the giant was just beginning to wake.

'I smell the flesh of a man!' murmured he, stretching his great arms.

'Why, how in the world could any man get down here?' asked the princess. 'You had better go to sleep again.'

So he turned over and went to sleep. Then the princess signed to Bensurdatu, who drew his sword and cut off the

giant's head with such a blow that it flew into the corner. The heart of the princess leapt within her and she placed a golden crown on the head of Bensurdatu and called him her deliverer.

'Now show me where your sisters are,' he said, 'that I may free them also.'

So the princess opened a door and led him into another hall, wherein sat her next sister also guarded by a giant who was fast asleep. When the second princess saw them, she made a sign to them to hide themselves, for the giant was showing symptoms of waking.

'I smell man's flesh!' murmured he, sleepily.

'Now, how could any man get down here?' asked she. 'Go to sleep again.' And as soon as he closed his eyes, Bensurdatu stole out from his corner, and struck such a blow that the giant's head flew far, far away. The princess could not find words to thank Bensurdatu for what he had done, and she too placed in his hand a golden crown.

'Now show me where your youngest sister is,' said he, 'that I may free her also.'

'Ah, that I fear you will never be able to do,' sighed they, 'for she is in the power of a serpent with seven heads.'

'Take me to him,' replied Bensurdatu. 'It will be a splendid fight.'

Then the princess opened a door. Bensurdatu passed through and found himself in a hall that was even larger than the other two. And there stood the youngest sister, chained fast to the wall. Before her was stretched a serpent with seven heads, horrible to see.

As Bensurdatu came forward it twisted all its seven heads in his direction and then made a quick dart to snatch him within its grasp. But Bensurdatu drew his sword and laid about him, till the seven heads were rolling on the floor. Flinging down his sword he rushed to the princess and broke her chains, while she wept for joy and embraced him, and took the golden crown from off her head and placed it in his hand.

'Now we must go back to the upper word,' said Bensurdatu, and led her to the bottom of the river. The other princesses were waiting there, and he tied the rope round the eldest and rang his bell. The knights above heard and drew her gently up. They then unfastened the rope and threw it back into the river, and in a few moments the second princess stood beside her sister.

So now there were left only Bensurdatu and the youngest princess. 'Dear Bensurdatu,' said she, 'do me a kindness and let them draw you up before me. I dread the treachery of the knights.'

'No, no,' replied Bensurdatu, 'I certainly will not leave you down here. There is nothing to fear from my comrades.'

'If it is your wish I will go up then; but first I swear that if you do not follow to marry me, I shall stay single for the rest of my life.'

Then he bound the rope round her, and the knights drew her up.

But instead of lowering the rope again into the river, envy at the courage and success of Bensurdatu so filled the hearts of the two knights that they turned away and left him to perish. And, more than that, they threatened the princesses and forced them to promise to tell their parents that it was the two knights who had set them free. 'And if they should ask you about Bensurdatu, you must say you have never seen him,' they added; and the princesses, fearing for their lives, promised everything, and they rode back to court together.

The king and queen were beside themselves with joy when

they saw their dear children once more. But when the knights had told their story and the dangers they had run, the king declared that they had gained their reward and the two eldest princesses should become their wives.

And now we must see what poor Bensurdatu was doing. He waited patiently a long, long time, but when the rope never came back he knew he had been wrong, and that his comrades had betrayed him.

'Ah, now I shall never reach the world again,' murmured he. But being a brave man and knowing that bemoaning his fate would profit him nothing, he rose and began to search through the three halls where, perhaps, he might find something to help him. In the last one stood a dish, covered with food, which reminded him that he was hungry, and he sat down and ate and drank.

Months passed away when, one morning, as he was walking through the halls, he noticed a purse hanging on the wall, which had never been there before. He took it down to examine it, and nearly let it fall with surprise when a voice came from the purse saying:

'What commands have you?'

'Oh, take me out of this horrible place, up into the world again.' And in a moment he was standing by the river bank, with the purse tightly grasped in his hand.

'Now let me have the most beautiful ship that ever was built, all manned and ready for sea.'

And there was the ship, with a flag floating from its mast on which were the words, *King with the three crowns*. Then Bensurdatu climbed on board and sailed away to the city where the three princesses dwelt; and when he reached the harbor he blew trumpets and beat drums, so every one ran to the doors and windows.

The king heard, too, and saw the beautiful vessel, and said to himself, 'That must indeed be a mighty monarch, for he has three crowns while I have only one.' So he hastened to greet the stranger, and invited him to his castle, for, thought he, this will be a fine husband for my youngest daughter. Now, the youngest princess had never married and had turned a deaf ear to all her wooers.

Such a long time had passed since Bensurdatu had left the palace, the king never guessed for a moment that the splendidly clad stranger before him was the man whom he had so deeply mourned as dead.

'Noble lord,' said he, 'let us feast and make merry together, and then, if it seem good to you, do me the honor to take my youngest daughter to wife.'

Bensurdatu was glad, and they all sat down to a great feast, and there were great rejoicings. But only the youngest daughter was sad, for her thoughts were with Bensurdatu. After they arose from the table the king said to her:

'Dear child, this mighty lord does you the honor to ask your hand in marriage.'

'Oh, father,' answered she, 'spare me, I pray you, for I desire to remain single.'

Then Bensurdatu turned to her, and said, 'And if I were Bensurdatu, would you give the same answer to me?'

As she stood silently gazing at him, he added, 'Yes, I am Bensurdatu, and this is my story.'

The king and queen had their hearts stirred within them at the tale of his adventures, and when he had ended the king stretched out his hand, and said:

'Dear Bensurdatu, my youngest daughter shall indeed be your wife, and when I die my crown shall be yours. As for the men who have betrayed you, they shall leave the country and you shall see them no more.'

The wedding feast was ordered, and rejoicings were held for three days over the marriage of Bensurdatu and the youngest princess.

[From the *Sicilianische Märchen*. L. Gonzenbach.]

The Bear

ONCE UPON A TIME
there was a king who had an only daughter. He was so proud
and so fond of her that he was in constant terror something
would happen to her if she went outside the palace, and thus,
owing to his great love for her, he forced her to lead the life of
a prisoner, shut up within her own rooms.

The princess did not like this at all and, one day, she complained about it very bitterly to her nurse. Now the nurse was
a witch, though the king did not know it. For some time she
listened and tried to soothe the princess; but when she saw that
she would not be comforted, she said to her:

'Your father loves you very dearly, as you know. Whatever
you were to ask from him he would give you. The one thing he
will not grant you is permission to leave the palace. Now, do as
I tell you. Go to your father and ask him to give you a wooden
wheelbarrow, and a bear's skin. When you have them bring
them to me and I will touch them with my magic wand. The
wheelbarrow will then move of itself and will take you at full
speed wherever you want to go, and the bear's skin will make
such a covering for you that no one will recognize you.'

So the princess did as the witch advised her. The king, when he heard her strange request, was greatly astonished and asked her what she meant to do with a wheelbarrow and a bear's skin. And the princess answered:

'You never let me leave the house—at least you might grant me this request.'

So the king granted it, and the princess went back to her nurse, taking the wheelbarrow and the bear's skin with her.

As soon as the witch saw them, she touched them with her magic wand, and in a moment the wheelbarrow began to move about in all directions. The princess next put on the bear's skin, which so completely changed her appearance that no one could have known she was a girl and not a bear. In this strange attire she seated herself on the wheelbarrow, and in a few minutes she found herself far away from the palace and moving rapidly through a great forest. Here she stopped the wheelbarrow with a sign that the witch had shown her, and hid herself and it in a thick grove of flowering shrubs.

Now it happened that the prince of that country was hunting with his dogs in the forest. Suddenly he caught sight of the bear hiding among the shrubs, and calling his dogs hounded them on to attack it. But the girl, seeing what peril she was in, cried:

'Call off your dogs, or they will kill me. What harm have I ever done to you?'

At these words, coming from a bear, the prince was so startled that for a moment he stood stock-still, then he said quite gently, 'Will you come with me? I will take you to my home.'

'I will come gladly,' replied the bear; and seating herself on the wheelbarrow it at once began to move in the direction of the prince's palace. You may imagine the surprise of the prince's mother when she saw her son return accompanied by a bear, who at once set about doing the housework better than any servant the queen had ever seen.

Now it happened that great festivities were going on in the palace of a neighboring prince, and at dinner, one day, the prince said to his mother, 'This evening there is to be a great ball, to which I must go.'

And his mother answered, 'Go and dance, and enjoy yourself.'

Suddenly a voice came from under the table, where the bear had rolled itself, as was its wont, 'Let me come to the ball; I, too, would like to dance.'

But the only answer the prince made was to give the bear a kick and drive it out of the room.

In the evening the prince set off for the ball. As soon as he had started, the bear came to the queen and implored to be allowed to go to the ball, saying that she would hide herself so well no one would know she was there. The kind-hearted queen could not refuse her.

Then the bear ran to her wheelbarrow, threw off her bear's skin, and touched it with the magic wand the witch had given her. In a moment the skin was changed into an exquisite ball dress woven out of moonbeams, and the wheelbarrow became a carriage drawn by two prancing steeds. Stepping into the carriage the princess drove to the grand entrance of the palace. When she entered the ballroom, in her wondrous dress of moonbeams, she looked so lovely, so different from all the other guests, that everyone wondered who she was, and no one could tell where she had come from.

From the moment he saw her, the prince fell desperately in love with her, and all the evening he would dance with no one but the beautiful stranger.

When the ball was over, the princess drove away in her

carriage at full speed, for she wished to reach home in time to change her ball dress into the bear's skin, and the carriage into the wheelbarrow, before anyone discovered who she was.

The prince, putting spurs into his horse, rode after her, for he was determined not to let her out of his sight. But suddenly a thick mist arose and hid her from him. When he reached his home he could talk to his mother of nothing else but the beautiful stranger with whom he had danced so often, and with whom he was so much in love.

And the bear beneath the table smiled to itself and muttered, 'I am the beautiful stranger. Oh, how I have taken you in!'

The next evening there was a second ball and, as you may believe, the prince was determined not to miss it, for he thought he would once more see the lovely girl, dance with her and talk to her, and make her talk to him, for at the first ball she had never opened her lips.

And, sure enough, as the music struck up the first dance, the beautiful stranger entered the room, looking even more radiant than the night before, for this time her dress was woven out of the rays of the sun. All evening the prince danced with her, but she never spoke a word.

When the ball was over he tried once more to follow her carriage, that he might know whence she came, but suddenly a great waterspout fell from the sky, and the blinding sheets of rain hid her from his sight.

When he reached his home he told his mother that he had again seen the lovely girl, and that this time she had been even more beautiful than the night before.

Again the bear smiled beneath the table, and muttered, 'I have taken him in a second time. He has no idea that I am the beautiful girl with whom he is so much in love.'

On the next evening, the prince returned to the palace for the third ball. And the princess went too, and this time she had changed her bear's skin into a dress woven out of the starlight, studded all over with gems, and she looked so dazzling and so beautiful, that everyone wondered, and said that no one so beautiful had ever been seen before. And the prince danced with her and, though he could not induce her to speak, he succeeded in slipping a ring on her finger.

When the ball was over, he followed her carriage, and rode at such a pace that for long he kept it in sight. Then suddenly a terrible wind arose between him and the carriage, and he could not overtake it.

When he reached his home he said to his mother, 'I do not know what is to become of me. I think I shall go mad, I am so much in love with that girl and I have no means of finding out who she is. I danced with her and gave her a ring, and yet I do not know her name nor where I am to find her.'

Then the bear laughed beneath the table and muttered to itself.

And the prince continued; 'I am tired to death. Order some soup to be made for me, but I don't want that bear to meddle with it. Every time I speak of my love the brute mutters and laughs, and seems to mock at me. I hate the sight of the creature!'

When the soup was ready, the bear brought it to the prince; but before handing it to him, she dropped into the plate the ring the prince had given her the night before at the ball. The prince began to eat his soup very slowly and languidly, for he was sad at heart, and all his thoughts were busy, wondering how and where he could see the lovely stranger again. Suddenly he noticed the ring at the bottom of the plate. In a moment he recognized it, and was dumb with surprise.

Then he saw the bear standing beside him, looking at him

with gentle, beseeching eyes, and something in the eyes of the bear made him say, 'Take off that skin, some mystery is hidden beneath it.'

And the bear's skin dropped off, and the beautiful girl stood before him, in the dress woven out of the starlight, and he saw that she was the stranger with whom he had fallen so deeply in love. And now she appeared to him a thousand times more beautiful than ever, and he led her to his mother. The princess told them her story, how she had been kept shut up by her father in his palace, and how she had wearied of her imprisonment. And the prince's mother loved her and rejoiced that her son should have so good and beautiful a wife.

So they were married, and lived happily for many years, and reigned wisely over their kingdom.

Bobino

ONCE UPON A TIME
there was a rich merchant who had an only son called Bobino.
Now, as the boy was clever and had a great desire for knowl-
edge, his father sent him to be under a master, from whom he
thought he would learn to speak all sorts of foreign languages.
After some years with this master, Bobino returned to his home.

One evening, as he and his father were walking in the garden,
the sparrows in the trees above their heads began such a twitter-
ing that they found it impossible to hear each other speak. This
annoyed the merchant very much, so, to soothe him, Bobino
said:

'Would you like me to explain to you what the sparrows are
saying to each other?'

The merchant looked at his son in astonishment, and answered, 'What can you mean? How can you explain what the
sparrows say? Do you consider yourself a soothsayer or a magician?'

'I am neither a soothsayer nor a magician,' answered Bobino,
'but my master taught me the language of all the animals.'

'Alas, for my good money!' exclaimed the merchant. 'The
master has certainly mistaken my intention. Of course I meant

you to learn the languages that human beings talk, not the language of animals.'

'Have patience,' answered the son. 'My master thought it best to begin with the language of animals, and later to learn the languages of human beings.'

On their way into the house the dog ran to meet them, barking furiously.

'What can be the matter with the beast?' asked the merchant. 'Why should he bark at me like that, when he knows me quite well?'

'Shall I explain to you what he is saying?' said Bobino.

'Leave me in peace; don't trouble me with your nonsense,' said the merchant quite crossly. 'How my money has been wasted!'

A little later, as they sat down to supper, some frogs in a neighboring pond set up such a croaking as had never been heard. The noise so irritated the merchant that he quite lost his temper and exclaimed:

'This only was wanting to add the last drop to my discomfort and disappointment.'

'Shall I explain to you?' began Bobino.

'Will you hold your tongue with your explanations?' shouted the merchant. 'Go to bed, and don't let me see your face again!'

So Bobino went to bed and slept soundly. But his father, who could not get over his disappointment at the waste of his money, was so angry, that he sent for two servants and gave them orders, which they were to carry out on the following day.

Next morning one of the servants awakened Bobino early and made him get into a carriage that was waiting for him. The servant placed himself on the seat beside him, while the other servant rode alongside the carriage as an escort. Bobino could not understand what they were going to do with him or where he was being taken; but he noticed that the servant beside him looked very sad and his eyes were swollen with crying.

Curious to know the reason he said to him, 'Why are you so sad? And where are you taking me?'

But the servant would say nothing. At last, moved by Bobino's entreaties, he said, 'My poor boy, I am taking you to your death and, what is worse, I am doing so by the order of your father.'

'But why,' exclaimed Bobino, 'does he want me to die? What evil have I done him, or what fault have I committed that he should wish to bring about my death?'

'You have done him no evil,' answered the servant, 'neither have you committed any fault. But he is half mad with anger because, in all these years of study, you have learned nothing but the language of animals. He expected something quite different from you, that is why he is determined you shall die.'

'If that is the case, kill me at once,' said Bobino. 'What is the use of waiting, if it must be done?'

'I have not the heart to do it,' answered the servant. 'I would rather think of some way of saving your life and, at the same time, of protecting ourselves from your father's anger. By good luck the dog has followed us. We will kill it, cut out the heart, and take it back to your father. He will believe it is yours, and you, in the meantime, will have made your escape.'

When they had reached the thickest part of the wood, Bobino got out of the carriage, and having said good-bye to the servants set out on his wanderings.

On and on he walked, till at last, late in the evening, he came to a house where some herdsmen lived. He knocked at the door and begged for shelter for the night. The herdsmen, seeing how gentle a youth he seemed, made him welcome and bade him sit down and share their supper.

While they were eating it, the dog in the courtyard began to bark. Bobino walked to the window, listened attentively for a minute, and then turning to the herdsmen said:

'Send your wives and daughters at once to bed, and arm yourselves as best you can, because at midnight a band of robbers will attack this house.'

The herdsmen were quite taken aback and thought the youth must have taken leave of his senses.

'How can you know,' they said, 'that a band of robbers means to attack us? Who told you so?'

'I know it from the dog's barking,' answered Bobino. 'I understand his language, and if I had not been here the poor beast would have wasted his breath to no purpose. You had better follow my advice, if you wish to save your lives and property.'

The herdsmen were more and more astonished, but they decided to do as Bobino advised. They sent their wives and daughters upstairs, then, having armed themselves, they took up their position behind a hedge, waiting for midnight.

Just as the clock struck twelve they heard the sound of approaching footsteps, and a band of robbers cautiously advanced toward the house. But the herdsmen were on the lookout; they sprang on the robbers from behind the hedge, and with blows from their cudgels soon put them to flight.

You may believe how grateful they were to Bobino, to whose timely warning they owed their safety. They begged him to stay and make his home with them, but as he wanted to see more of the world, he thanked them warmly for their hospitality, and set out once more on his wanderings.

All day he walked, and in the evening he came to a peasant's house. While he was wondering whether he should knock and ask shelter for the night, he heard a great croaking of frogs in a ditch behind the house. Stepping to the back he saw a very strange sight. Four frogs were throwing a small bottle about from one to the other, making a great croaking as they did so.

Bobino listened for a few minutes, and then knocked at the door of the house. It was opened by the peasant, who asked him to come in and have some supper.

When the meal was over, his host told him that they were in great trouble as his eldest daughter was so ill they feared she could not recover. A great doctor, who had been passing that way some time before, had promised to send her some medicine that would have cured her, but the servant to whom he had entrusted the medicine had let it drop on the way back, and now there seemed no hope for the girl.

Then Bobino told the father of the small bottle he had seen the frogs play with and that he knew it was the medicine the doctor had sent to the girl. The peasant asked him how he could be sure of this, and Bobino explained to him that he understood the language of animals and had heard what the frogs said as they tossed the bottle about.

So the peasant fetched the bottle from the ditch and gave the medicine to his daughter. In the morning she was much better and the grateful father did not know how to thank Bobino enough. But Bobino would accept nothing from him and, having said good-bye, set out once more on his wanderings.

One day, soon after this, he came upon two men resting under a tree in the heat of the day. Being tired he stretched himself on the ground at no great distance from them, and soon they all three began to talk to one another. In the course of conversation, Bobino asked the two men where they were going; and they replied that they were on their way to a neighboring town where, that day, a new ruler was to be chosen by the people.

While they were still talking, some sparrows settled on the tree under which they were lying. Bobino was silent, and ap-

peared to be listening attentively. At the end of a few minutes
he said to his companions:

'Do you know what those sparrows are saying? They are saying that today one of us will be chosen ruler of that town.'

The men said nothing but looked at each other. A few minutes later, seeing that Bobino had fallen asleep, they stole away,
and made with all haste for the town, where the election of a
new ruler was to take place.

A great crowd was assembled in the market place, waiting
for the hour when an eagle should be let loose from a cage, for
it had been settled that on whosoever's house the eagle alighted,
the owner of that house should become ruler of the town.

At last the hour arrived; the eagle was set free, and all eyes
were strained to see where it would alight. But circling over the
heads of the crowd, it flew straight in the direction of a young
man, who was at that moment entering the town. This was
none other than Bobino, who had awakened soon after his companions had left him and had followed in their footsteps.

All the people shouted and proclaimed that he was their
future ruler, and he was conducted by a great crowd to the
governor's house, which was for the future to be his home.
And here he lived happily and ruled wisely over the people.

Father Grumbler

ONCE UPON A TIME there lived a man who had nearly as many children as there were sparrows in the garden. He had to work very hard all day to get them enough to eat, and was often tired and cross, and so abused everything and everybody that people called him 'Father Grumbler.'

By-and-by he grew weary of always working, and on Sundays he lay a long while in bed, instead of going to church. Then after a time he found it dull to sit so many hours by himself, thinking of nothing but how to pay the rent that was owing, and as the tavern across the road looked bright and cheerful, he walked in one day and sat down with his friends. 'It was just to chase away Care,' he said, but when he came out, hours and hours afterward, Care came out with him.

Father Grumbler entered his house feeling more dismal than when he left it, for he knew that he had wasted both his time and money.

'I will go and see the Holy Man in the cave near the well,' he said to himself. 'Perhaps he can tell me why all the luck is for other people, and only misfortunes happen to me.' And he set out at once for the cave.

It was a long way off, and the road led over mountains and through valleys. But at last he reached the cave where the Holy Man dwelt and knocked at the door.

'Who is there?' asked a voice from within. 'It is I, Holy Man. Father Grumbler, you know, who has as many children as sparrows in the garden.'

'Well, and what is it that you want?'

'I want to know why other people have all the luck, and only misfortunes happen to me!'

The Holy Man did not answer, but went into an inner cave, from which he came out, bearing something in his hand.

'Do you see this basket?' said he. 'It is a magical basket, and if you are hungry you have only to say, "Little Basket, little basket, do your duty," and you will eat the best dinner you ever had in your life. But when you have had enough, be sure you don't forget to cry out, "That will do for today." Oh—and one thing more—you need not show it to everybody and declare that I have given it to you. Do you understand?'

Father Grumbler was always accustomed to think of himself as so unlucky that he did not know whether the Holy Man was not playing a trick upon him, but he took the basket without being polite enough to say either 'Thank you,' or 'Good morning,' and went away. However, he only waited till he was out of sight of the cave before he stooped down and whispered:

'Little basket, little basket, do your duty.'

Now the basket had a lid so he could not see what was inside, but he heard quite clearly strange noises, as if a sort of scuffling was going on. Then the lid burst open, and a quantity of delicious little white rolls came tumbling out, one after the other, followed by a stream of small fishes all ready cooked. What a quantity there were to be sure! The whole road was covered with them, and the banks on each side were beginning to disappear. Father Grumbler felt quite frightened at the torrent, but at last he remembered what the Holy Man had told him, and cried at the top of his voice:

'Enough! Enough! That will do for today!' And the lid of the basket closed with a snap.

Father Grumbler sighed with relief and happiness as he looked around him, and sitting down on a heap of stones, he ate till he could eat no more. Trout, salmon, turbot, soles, and a hundred other fishes whose names he did not know, lay boiled, fried and grilled within reach of his hands. As the Holy Man had said, he had never eaten such a dinner; still, when he had done, he shook his head and grumbled:

'Yes, there is plenty to eat, of course, but it only makes me thirsty, and there is not a drop to drink anywhere.'

Yet, somehow, he could never tell why, he looked up and saw the tavern in front of him, which he thought was miles and miles and miles away.

'Bring the best wine you have and two glasses, good mother,' he said as he entered, 'and if you are fond of fish there is enough here to feed the house. Only there is no need to chatter about it all over the place. You understand? Eh?'

And without waiting for an answer he whispered to the basket; 'Little basket, little basket, do your duty.'

The innkeeper and his wife thought their customer had gone suddenly mad, and watched him closely, ready to spring on him if he became violent; but both instinctively jumped backward, nearly into the fire, as rolls and fishes of every kind came tumbling out of the basket, covering the tables and chairs and the floor, and even overflowing into the street.

'Be quick, be quick, and pick them up,' cried the man. 'And if these are not enough, there are plenty more to be had for the asking.'

The innkeeper and his wife did not need telling twice. Down they went on their knees and gathered up everything they could lay hands on. But busy though they seemed, they found time to whisper to each other:

'If we can only get hold of that basket it will make our fortune!'

So they began by inviting Father Grumbler to sit down to the table, and brought out the best wine in the cellar, hoping it might loosen his tongue. But Father Grumbler was wiser than they gave him credit for, and though they tried in all manner of ways to find out who had given him the basket, he put them off, and kept his secret to himself.

Unluckily, though he did not speak, he did drink, and it was not long before he fell fast asleep. Then the woman fetched from her kitchen a basket, so like the magic one that no one, without looking very closely, could tell the difference, and placed it in Father Grumbler's hand, while she hid the other carefully away.

It was dinner time when the man awoke and, jumping up hastily, he set out for home, where he found all the children gathered round a basin of thin soup, and pushing their wooden bowls forward, hoping to have the first spoonful. Their father burst into the midst of them, bearing his basket, and crying:

'Don't spoil your appetites, children, with that stuff. Do you see this basket? Well, I have only to say, "Little basket, little basket, do your duty," and you will see what will happen. Now you shall say it instead of me, for a treat.'

The children, wondering and delighted, repeated the words, but nothing happened. Again and again they tried but the basket was only a basket, with a few scales of fish sticking to the bottom, for the innkeeper's wife had taken it to market the day before.

'What is the matter with the thing?' cried the father at last, snatching the basket from them, and turning it over, grumbling while he did so, under the eyes of his astonished wife and children, who did not know whether to cry or to laugh.

'It certainly smells of fish,' he said, and then he stopped, for a sudden thought had come to him.

'Suppose it is not mine at all; supposing—Ah, the scoundrels!'

And without listening to his wife and children, who were frightened at his strange conduct and begged him to stay at home, he ran across to the tavern and burst open the door.

'Can I do anything for you, Father Grumbler?' asked the innkeeper's wife in her softest voice.

'I have taken the wrong basket—by mistake, of course,' said he. 'Here is yours, will you give me back my own?'

'Why, what are you talking about?' answered she. 'You can see for yourself that there is no basket here.'

And though Father Grumbler did look, it was quite true that none was to be seen.

'Come, take a glass to warm you this cold day,' said the woman, who was anxious to keep him in a good temper, and as this was an invitation Father Grumbler never refused, he tossed it off and left the house.

He took the road that led to the Holy Man's cave, and made such haste that it was not long before he reached it.

'Who is there?' asked a voice in answer to his knock.

'It is me, it is me, Holy Man. You know quite well. Father Grumbler, who has as many children as sparrows in the garden.'

'But, my good man, it was only yesterday that I gave you a handsome present.'

'Yes, Holy Man, and here it is. But something has happened, I don't know what, and it won't work any more.'

'Well, put it down. I will go and see if I can find anything for you.'

In a few minutes the Holy Man returned with a cock under his arm.

'Listen to me,' he said, 'whenever you want money, you have only to say, "Show me what you can do, cock," and you will see some wonderful things. But, remember, it is not necessary to let all the world into the secret.'

'Oh no, Holy Man, I am not so foolish as that.'

'Nor to tell everybody that I gave it to you,' went on the Holy Man. 'I do not have these treasures by the dozen.'

And without waiting for an answer he shut the door.

As before, the distance seemed to have wonderfully shortened, and in a moment the tavern rose up in front of Father Grumbler. Without stopping to think, he went straight in and found the innkeeper's wife in the kitchen making a cake.

'Where have you come from, with that fine red cock in your basket,' asked she, for the bird was so big that the lid would not shut down properly.

'Oh, I come from a place where they don't keep these things by the dozen,' he replied, sitting down in front of the table.

The woman said no more, but set before him a bottle of his favorite wine, and soon he began to wish to display his prize.

'Show me what you can do, cock,' cried he. And the cock stood up and flapped his wings three times, crowing 'coquerico' with a voice like a trumpet, and at each crow there fell from his beak golden drops, and diamonds as large as peas.

This time Father Grumbler did not invite the innkeeper's wife to pick up his treasures, but put his own hat under the cock's beak to catch everything he let fall. And he did not see the husband and wife exchanging glances with each other which said, 'That would be a splendid cock to put with our basket.'

'Have another glass of wine?' suggested the innkeeper, when they had finished admiring the beauty of the cock, for they pretended not to have seen the gold or the diamonds. And Father Grumbler, nothing loth, drank one glass after another, till his head fell forward on the table, and once more he was sound asleep. Then the woman gently coaxed the cock from the basket and carried it off to her own poultry yard, from which she brought one exactly like it, and popped it in its place.

Night was falling when the man awoke, and throwing proudly some grains of gold on the table to pay for the wine he had drunk, he tucked the cock comfortably into his basket and set out for home.

His wife and all the children were waiting for him at the door, and as soon as she caught sight of him she cried out:

'You are a nice man to go wasting your time and your money, drinking in that tavern, and leaving us to starve! Aren't you ashamed of yourself?'

'You don't know what you are talking of,' he answered. 'Money? Why, I have gold and diamonds now, as much as I want. Do you see that cock? Well, you have only to say to him, "Show me what you can do, cock," and something splendid will happen.'

Neither wife nor children were inclined to put much faith in him after their last experience; however, they thought it was worth trying and did as he told them. The cock flew round the room like a mad thing and crowed till their heads nearly split with the noise, but no gold or diamonds dropped on the brick floor—not the tiniest grain of either.

Father Grumbler stared in silence for an instant, and then he began to swear so loudly that even his family, accustomed as they were to his language, wondered at him.

At last he grew a little quieter, but remained as puzzled as ever.

'Can I have forgotten the words? But I know that was what he said! And I saw the diamonds with my own eyes!'

Then suddenly he seized the cock, shut it into the basket, and rushed out of the house. His heavy wooden shoes clattered as he ran along the road, and he made such haste that the stars were only just beginning to come out when he reached the cave of the Holy Man.

'Who is that knocking?' asked a voice from within.

'It is me! It is me! Holy Man, you know! Father—'

'But, my good fellow, you really should give someone else a chance. This is the third time you have come—and at such an hour, too!'

'Oh, yes, Holy Man, I know it is very late, but you will forgive me! It is your cock—there is something the matter. It is like the basket. Look!'

'That my cock? That my basket? Somebody has played you a trick, my good man!'

'A trick?' repeated Father Grumbler, who began to understand what had happened. 'Then it must have been those two—'

'I warned you not to show them to anybody,' said the Holy Man. 'You deserve—but I will give you one more chance.' And, turning, he unhooked something from the wall.

'When you wish to dust your own jacket or those of your friends,' he said, 'you have only got to say, "Flack! Flick! Switch, be quick," and you will see what happens. That is all

I have to tell you.' And, smiling to himself, the Holy Man pushed Father Grumbler out of the cave.

'Ah, I understand now,' muttered the good man, as he took the road home, 'but I think I have you two rascals!' And he hurried on to the tavern with his basket under his arm, and the cock and the switch both inside.

'Good evening, friends!' he said, as he entered the inn. 'I am very hungry, and should be glad if you would roast this cock for me as soon as possible. This cock and no other—mind what I say,' he went on. 'Oh, and another thing! You can light the fire with this basket. When you have done that I will show you something I have in my bag,' and, as he spoke, he tried to imitate the smile that the Holy Man had given him.

These directions made the innkeeper's wife very uneasy. However, she said nothing, and began to roast the cock, while her husband did his best to make the man sleepy with wine, but all in vain.

After dinner, which he did not eat without grumbling, for the cock was very tough, the man struck his hand on the table, and said:

'Now listen to me. Go and fetch my cock and my basket, at once. Do you hear?'

'Your cock, and your basket, Father Grumbler? But you have just—'

'My cock and my basket!' interrupted he. 'And, if you are too deaf and too stupid to understand what that means, I have something which may help to teach you.' And opening the bag, he cried, 'Flack! Flick! Switch, be quick.'

And flack! Flick! Like lightning a white switch sprang out of the bag, and gave such hearty blows to the innkeeper and his wife, and to Father Grumbler into the bargain, that they all jumped as high as feathers when a mattress is shaken.

'Stop! Stop! Make it stop, and you shall have back your cock and basket,' cried the man and his wife. And Father Grumbler, who had no wish to go on, called out between his hops:

'Stop then, can't you? That is enough for today!'

But the switch paid no attention, and dealt out its blows as before, and might have been dealing them to this day, if the Holy Man had not heard their cries and come to the rescue. 'Into the bag, quick!' said he, and the switch obeyed.

'Now go and fetch me the cock and the basket.' And the woman went without a word, and placed them on the table.

'You have all got what you deserved,' continued the Holy Man, 'and I have no pity for any of you. I shall take my treasures home, and perhaps some day I may find a man who knows how to make the best of the chances that are given him. But that will never be you,' he added, turning to Father Grumbler.

[From *Les Contes Populaires*.]

The Knights of the Fish

ONCE UPON A TIME there lived an old cobbler who worked hard at his trade from morning till night, and scarcely gave himself a moment to eat. But, industrious as he was, he could hardly buy bread and cheese for himself and his wife, and they grew thinner and thinner daily.

For a long while they pretended to each other that they had no appetite, and that a few blackberries from the hedges were a great deal nicer than a good strong bowl of soup. But at length, there came a day when the cobbler could bear it no longer, and he threw away his last and, borrowing a rod from a neighbor, he went out to fish.

Now the cobbler was as patient about fishing as he had been about cobbling. From dawn to dark he stood on the banks of the little stream, without hooking anything better than an eel, or a few old shoes, that even he, clever though he was, felt were not worth mending. At length his patience began to give way, and as he undressed one night he said to himself:

'Well, I will give it one more chance, and if I don't catch a fish tomorrow, I will go and hang myself.'

He had not cast his line for ten minutes the next morning before he drew from the river the most beautiful fish he had ever seen in his life. But he nearly fell into the water from surprise, when the fish began to speak to him in a small, squeaky voice:

'Take me back to your hut and cook me; then cut me up and sprinkle me over with pepper and salt. Give two of the pieces to your wife, and bury two more in the garden.'

The cobbler did not know what to make of these strange words; but he was wiser than many people, and when he did not understand, he thought it was well to obey. His children wanted to eat all the fish themselves, and begged their father to tell them what to do with the pieces he had put aside; but the cobbler only laughed and told them it was no business of theirs. And when they were safe in bed he stole out and buried the two pieces in the garden.

By and by two babies, exactly alike, lay in a cradle, and in the garden were two tall plants, with two brilliant shields on the top.

Years passed away, and the babies were almost men. They were tired of living quietly at home, being mistaken for each other by everybody they saw, and determined to set off in different directions, to seek adventures.

So, one fine morning, the two brothers left the hut and walked together to the place where the great road divided. There they embraced and parted, promising that if anything remarkable happened to either, he would return to the cross roads and wait till his brother came.

The youth who took the path that ran eastward arrived presently at a large city where he found everybody standing at the doors, wringing their hands and weeping bitterly.

'What is the matter?' asked he, pausing and looking round. And a man replied, in a faltering voice, that each year a beautiful girl was chosen by lot to be offered up to a dreadful fiery dragon, who had a mother even worse than himself, and this year the lot had fallen on their peerless princess.

'But where is the princess?' asked the young man.

And again the man answered him, 'She is standing under a tree, a mile away, waiting for the dragon.'

This time the Knight of the Fish did not stop to hear more, but ran as fast as he could, and found the princess bathed in tears and trembling from head to foot.

She turned as she heard the sound of his sword and removed her handkerchief from her eyes.

'Fly!' she cried. 'Fly while you have yet time, before that monster sees you.'

She said it, and she meant it; yet, when he had turned his back, she felt more forsaken than before. But in reality it was not more than a few minutes before he came back, galloping furiously on a horse he had borrowed, and carrying a huge mirror across its neck.

'I am in time, then!' he cried, dismounting very carefully, and placing the mirror against the trunk of a tree.

'Give me your veil,' he said hastily to the princess. And when she had unwound it from her head he covered the mirror with it.

'The moment the dragon comes near you, you must tear off the veil,' cried he; 'and be sure you hide behind the tree. Have no fear; I shall be at hand.'

He and his horse had scarcely found shelter amongst some rocks, when the flap of the dragon's wings could be plainly heard. He tossed his head with delight at the sight of the princess, and approached slowly to the place where she stood, a little in front of the mirror. Then, still looking the monster steadily in the face, she passed one hand behind her back and

snatched off the veil, stepping swiftly behind the tree as she did so.

The princess had not known, when she obeyed the orders of the Knight of the Fish, what she expected to happen. Would the dragon with snaky locks be turned to stone, she wondered, like the dragon in an old story her nurse had told her; or would some fiery spark dart from the heart of the mirror and strike him dead?

Neither of these things occurred, but, instead, the dragon stopped short with surprise and rage when he saw a monster before him as big and strong as himself. He shook his mane with fury; the enemy in front did exactly the same. He lashed his tail, and rolled his red eyes, and the dragon opposite was no whit behind him. Opening his mouth to its very widest, he gave an awful roar; but the other dragon only roared back.

This was too much, and with another roar, which made the princess shake in her shoes, he flung himself upon his foe. In an instant the mirror lay at his feet broken into a thousand pieces, but as every piece reflected part of himself, the dragon thought that he too had been smashed into atoms.

It was the moment for which the Knight of the Fish had watched and waited, and before the dragon could find out that he was not hurt at all, the young man's lance was down his throat, and he was rolling, dead, on the grass.

Oh, what shouts of joy rang through the great city, when the youth came riding back, with the princess sitting behind him, and dragging the horrible monster by a rope. Everybody cried out that the king must give the victor the hand of the princess; and so he did, and no one had ever seen such balls and feasts and sports before. And when they were all over the young couple went to the palace prepared for them, which was so large that it was three miles round.

The first wet day after their marriage the bridegroom begged the bride to show him all the rooms in the palace, and it was so big and took so long that the sun was shining brightly again before they stepped on to the roof to see the view.

'What castle is that out there?' asked the knight; 'it seems to be made of black marble.'

'It is called the castle of Albatroz,' answered the princess. 'It is enchanted, and no one who has tried to enter it has ever come back.'

Her husband said nothing, and began to talk of something else. But the next morning he ordered his horse, took his spear, called his bloodhound, and set off for the castle.

It needed a brave man to approach it, for it made your hair stand on end merely to look at it; it was as dark as the night of a storm, and as silent as the grave. But the Knight of the Fish knew no fear and had never turned his back on an enemy, so he drew out his horn and blew a blast.

The sound awoke all the sleeping echoes in the castle, and was repeated now loudly, now softly, now near and now far. But nobody stirred for all that.

'Is there anyone inside?' cried the young man in his loudest voice. 'Anyone who will give a knight hospitality? Neither governor, nor squire, not even a page?'

'Not even a page!' answered the echoes. But the young man did not heed them and only struck a furious blow at the gate.

Then a small grating opened, and there appeared the tip of a huge nose, which belonged to the ugliest old woman that ever was seen.

'What do you want?' asked she.

'To enter,' he answered shortly. 'Can I rest here this night? Yes or no?'

'No, no, no!' repeated the echoes.

Between the fierce sun and his anger at being kept waiting, the Knight of the Fish had grown so hot that he lifted his visor, and, when the old woman saw how handsome he was, she began fumbling with the lock of the gate.

'Come in, come in,' said she, 'so fine a gentleman will do us no harm.'

'Harm!' repeated the echoes, but again the young man paid no heed.

'Let us go in, ancient dame,' he said, but she interrupted him.

'You must call me the Lady Berberisca,' she answered sharply. 'This is my castle, to which I bid you welcome. You shall live here with me and be my husband.' But at these words the knight let his spear fall, so surprised was he.

'I marry you? Why, you must be a hundred at least!' cried he. 'You are mad! All I desire is to inspect the castle and then go.' As he spoke he heard the voices give a mocking laugh; but the old woman took no notice, and only bade the knight follow her.

Old though she was, it seemed impossible to tire her. There was no room, however small, she did not lead him into, and each room was full of curious things he had never seen before.

At length they came to a stone staircase, which was so dark that you could not see your hand if you held it up before your face.

'I have kept my most precious treasure till the last,' said the old woman; 'but let me go first, for the stairs are steep, and you might easily break your leg.' So on she went, now and then calling back to the young man in the darkness. But he did not know that she had slipped aside into a recess, until suddenly he put his foot on a trap door which gave way under him, and he fell down, down, as many good knights had done before him, and his voice joined the echoes of theirs.

'So you would not marry me!' chuckled the old witch. 'Ha, ha! Ha, ha!'

MEANWHILE his brother had traveled far and wide, and at last he wandered back to the same great city where the other young knight had met with so many adventures. He noticed, with amazement, that as he walked through the streets the guards drew themselves up in line and saluted him, and the drummers played the royal march. But he was still more bewildered when several servants in livery ran up to him and told him that the princess was sure something terrible had befallen him and had made herself ill with weeping. At last it occurred to him that once more he had been taken for his brother. I had better say nothing, thought he, perhaps I shall be able to help him after all.

So he suffered himself to be borne in triumph to the palace, where the princess threw herself into his arms.

'And so you did go to the castle?' she asked.

'Yes, of course I did,' answered he.

'And what did you see there?'

'I am forbidden to tell you anything about it, until I have returned there once more,' replied he.

'Must you really go back to that dreadful place?' she asked wistfully. 'You are the only man who has ever come back from it.'

'I must,' was all he answered.

And the princess, who was a wise woman, only said, 'Well, go to bed now, for I am sure you must be very tired.'

But the knight shook his head. 'I have sworn never to lie in a bed as long as my work in the castle remains standing.'

The princess again sighed and was silent.

Early next day the young man started for the castle, feeling sure that some terrible thing must have happened to his brother.

At the blast of his horn the long nose of the old woman appeared at the grating, but the moment she caught sight of his face, she nearly fainted from fright, as she thought it was the ghost of the youth whose bones were lying in the dungeon of the castle.

'Lady of all the ages,' cried the newcomer, 'did you not give hospitality to a young knight but a short time ago?'

'A short time ago!' wailed the voices.

'And how have you ill-treated him?' he went on.

'Ill-treated him!' answered the voices. The woman did not stop to hear more. She turned to fly, but the knight's sword entered her body.

'Where is my brother, cruel hag?' asked he sternly.

'I will tell you,' said she, 'but as I feel that I am going to die, I shall keep that piece of news to myself till you have brought me to life again.'

The young man laughed scornfully. 'How do you propose that I should work that miracle?'

'Oh, it is quite easy. Go into the garden and gather the flowers of the everlasting plant and some of dragon's blood. Crush them together and boil them in a large tub of water, and then put me into it.'

The knight did as the old witch bade him and, sure enough, she came out quite whole, but uglier than ever. She then told the young man what had become of his brother, and he went down into the dungeon, and brought up his body and the bodies of the other victims who lay there, and when they were all washed in the magic water their strength was restored to them.

And, besides these, he found in another cavern the bodies of the girls who had been sacrificed to the dragon, and brought them back to life also.

As to the old witch, in the end she died of rage at seeing her prey escape her, and at the moment she drew her last breath the castle of Albatroz fell into ruins with a great noise.

[From *Cuentos, Oraciones, Adivinas recogidos* by Fernan Caballaro.]

The Seven Who Helped

LONG AGO THERE LIVED a very rich man who had three sons. When he felt himself to be dying he divided his property between them, making them share alike, both in money and lands. Soon after the man died, the king set forth a proclamation through the whole country that whoever could build a ship that should float both on land and sea should have his daughter to wife.

The eldest brother, when he heard it, said to the others, 'I think I will spend some of my money in trying to build that ship. I should like to have the king for my father-in-law.'

So he called together all the shipbuilders in the land and gave them orders to begin the ship without delay. Trees were cut down. And great preparations made, and in a few days everybody knew what it was all for, and there was a crowd of old people pressing round the gates of the yard, where the young man spent the most of his day.

'Ah, master, give us work,' they said, 'so we may earn our bread.'

But he only gave them hard words and spoke roughly to them. 'You are old and have lost your strength. Of what use are you?' And he drove them away.

Then came some boys and prayed him, 'Master, give us work.'

But he answered them, 'Of what use can you be, weaklings as you are! Get you gone!'

And if any presented themselves who were not skilled workmen he would have none of them.

At last there knocked at the gate a little old man with a long white beard, and said, 'Will you give me work so I may earn my bread?'

But he was driven away like the rest.

The ship took a long while to build and cost a great deal of money. When it was launched a sudden squall rose, and it fell to pieces, and with it all the young man's hopes of winning the princess. By this time he had not a penny left, so he went back to his two brothers and told his tale.

Then the second brother said to himself, as he listened, 'Certainly he has managed very badly, but I should like to see if I can't do better and win the princess for my own self.'

So he called together all the shipbuilders throughout the country and gave them orders to build a ship which should float on the land as well as on the sea. But his heart was no softer than his brother's, and every man who was not a skilled workman was chased away with hard words. Last came the white-bearded man, but he fared no better than the rest.

When the ship was finished the launching took place, and everything seemed going smoothly, when a gale sprang up, and the vessel was dashed to pieces on the rocks. The young man had spent his whole fortune on it, and now it was all swallowed up and he was forced to beg shelter from his youngest brother. When he told his story, the youngest said to himself:

'I am not rich enough to support us all three. I had better take my turn, and if I manage to win the princess there will be her fortune as well as my own for us to live on.'

So he called together all the shipbuilders in the kingdom and gave orders that a new ship should be built. Then all the old people came and asked for work, and he answered them cheerfully:

'Oh, yes, there is plenty for everybody.'

When the boys begged to be allowed to help he found something that they could do. And when the old man with the long white beard stood before him, praying that he might earn his bread, he replied:

'Oh, father, I could not suffer you to work, but you shall be overseer and look after the rest.'

Now the old man was a holy hermit and, when he saw how kind-hearted the youth was, he determined to do all he could to help him gain the wish of his heart.

By-and-by, when the ship was finished, the hermit said to his young friend, 'Now you can go and claim the king's daughter, for the ship will float both by land and sea.'

'Oh, good father,' cried the young man, 'you will not forsake me? Stay with me, I pray you, and lead me to the king!'

'If you wish it, I will,' said the hermit, 'on condition that you will give me half of anything you get.'

'Oh, if that is all, it is easily promised!' And they set out together on the ship.

After they had gone some distance they saw a man standing in a thick fog, which he was trying to put into a sack.

'Oh, good father,' exclaimed the youth, 'what can he be doing?'

'Ask him,' said the old man.

'What are you doing, my fine fellow?'

'I am putting the fog into my sack. That is my business.'

'Ask him if he will come with us,' whispered the hermit.

And the man answered, 'If you will give me enough to eat and drink I will gladly stay with you.'

So they took him on their ship, and the youth said, as they started off again, 'Good father, before we were two, and now we are three!'

After they had traveled a little farther they met a man who had torn up half the forest and was carrying all the trees on his shoulders.

'Good father,' exclaimed the youth, 'only look! Why has he done that?'

'Ask him why he has torn up all those trees.'

And the man replied, 'Oh, I've merely been gathering a handful of brushwood.'

'Beg him to come with us,' whispered the hermit.

And the strong man answered, 'Willingly, as long as you give me enough to eat and drink.' And he came on the ship.

Then the youth said to the hermit, 'Good father, before we were three, and now we are four.'

The ship traveled on again, and some miles farther along they saw a man drinking out of a stream till he had nearly drunk it dry.

'Good father,' said the youth, 'just look at that man! Did you ever see anybody drink like that?'

'Ask him why he does it,' answered the hermit.

'Why, there is nothing very odd in taking a mouthful of water!' replied the man, standing up.

'Beg him to come with us.' And the youth did so.

'With pleasure, as long as you give me enough to eat and drink.'

The youth whispered to the hermit, 'Good father, before we were four, and now we are five.'

A little way along they noticed another man in the middle of a stream, who was shooting into the water.

'Good father,' said the youth, 'what can he be shooting at?'

'Ask him,' answered the hermit.

'Hush, hush!' cried the man. Now you have frightened it away. In the Underworld sits a quail on a tree and I wanted to shoot it. That is my business. I hit everything I aim at.'

'Ask him if he will come with us.'

And the man replied, 'With all my heart, as long as I get enough to eat and drink.'

So they took him into the ship, and the young man whispered:

'Good father, before we were five, and now we are six.'

Off they went again, and before they had gone far they met a man striding toward them whose steps were so long that while one foot was on the north of the island the other was right down in the south.

'Good father, look at him! What long steps he takes!'

'Ask him why he does it,' replied the hermit.

'Oh, I am only going out for a little walk,' answered he.

'Ask him if he will come with us.'

'Gladly, if you will give me as much as I want to eat and drink,' said he, climbing up into the ship.

And the young man whispered, 'Good father, before we were six, and now we are seven.'

But the hermit knew what he was about, and why he gathered these strange people into the ship.

After many days, at last they reached the town where lived the king and his daughter. They stopped the vessel right in front of the palace, and the young man went in and bowed low before the king.

'O Majesty, I have done your bidding, and now is the ship

built that can travel over land and sea. Give me my reward and
let me have your daughter to wife.'

But the king said to himself, 'What! Am I to wed my
daughter to a man of whom I know nothing? Not even whether
he be rich or poor—a knight or a beggar?'

And aloud he spake, 'It is not enough that you have managed
to build the ship. You must find a runner who shall take this
letter to the ruler of the Underworld and bring me the answer
back in an hour.'

'That is not in the bond,' answered the young man.

'Well, do as you like,' replied the king, 'only you will not get
my daughter.'

The young man went out, sorely troubled, to tell his old
friend what had happened.

'Silly boy!' cried the hermit. 'Accept his terms at once, and
send off the long-legged man with the letter. He will take it in
no time at all.'

The youth's heart leapt for joy, and he returned to the king.
'Majesty, I accept your terms. Here is the messenger who will
do what you wish.'

The king had no choice but to give the man the letter,
and he strode off, making short work of the distance that lay
between the palace and the Underworld. He soon found the
ruler, who looked at the letter, and said to him, 'Wait a little
while I write the answer.' The man was so tired from his quick
walk that he went sound asleep and forgot all about his errand.

All this time the youth was anxiously counting the minutes
till he could get back and stood with his eyes fixed on the road
down which his messenger must come.

'What can be keeping him?' he said to the hermit when the
hour was nearly up.

Then the hermit sent for the man who could hit everything he aimed at, and said to him, 'Just see why the messenger stays so long.'

'Oh, he is sound asleep in the palace of the Underworld. However, I can soon wake him.'

Then he drew his bow and shot an arrow straight into the man's knee. The messenger awoke with a start, and when he saw that the hour had almost run out he snatched up the answer and rushed back with such speed that the clock had not yet struck when he entered the palace.

Now the young man thought he was sure of his bride, but the king said, 'Still you have not done enough. Before I give you my daughter you must find a man who can drink half the contents of my cellar in one day.'

'That is not in the bond,' complained the poor youth.

'Well, do as you like, only you will not get my daughter.'

The young man went sadly out and asked the hermit what he was to do.

'Silly boy!' said he. 'Why, tell the man who drinks up everything to do it.'

So they sent for the man, and said, 'Do you think you are able to drink half the royal cellar in one day?'

'Dear me, yes, and as much more as you want,' answered he. 'I am never satisfied.'

The king was not pleased when the young man agreed so readily, but he had no choice and ordered the servant to be taken downstairs. Oh, how he enjoyed himself! All day long he drank and drank and drank till, instead of half the cellar, he had drunk the whole, and there was not a cask but what stood empty.

And when the king saw this he said to the youth, 'You have

conquered, and I can no longer withhold my daughter. But, as her dowry, I shall give only so much as one man can carry away.'

'But,' answered the youth, 'let a man be ever so strong, he cannot carry more than a hundredweight, and what is that for a king's daughter?'

'Well, do as you like; I have said my say. It is your affair— not mine.'

The young man was puzzled and did not know what to reply, for though he would gladly have married the princess without a sixpence, he had spent all his money in building the ship and knew he could not give her all she wanted. So he went to the hermit and said to him:

'The king will only give for the princess' dowry as much as a man can carry. I have no money of my own left, and my brothers have none either.'

'Silly boy! Why, you have only to fetch the man who carried half the forest on his shoulders.'

The youth was glad, and called the strong man and told him what he must do. 'Take everything you can, till you are bent double. Never mind if you leave the palace bare.'

The strong man promised and nobly kept his word. He piled all he could see on his back—chairs, tables, wardrobes, chests of gold and silver—till there was nothing left. At last he took the king's crown and put it on the top. Then he carried his burden to the ship and stowed his treasures away, and the youth followed, leading the king's daughter.

But the king was left raging in his empty palace, and he called together his army and got ready his ships of war, in order that he might go after the vessel and bring back what had been taken away. The king's ships sailed very fast and soon caught up with the little vessel, and the sailors all shouted for joy.

Then the hermit looked out and saw how near they were, and he said to the youth, 'Do you see that?'

The youth shrieked, and cried, 'Ah, good father, it is a fleet of ships and they are chasing us; in a few moments they will be upon us.'

But the hermit bade him call the man who had the fog in his sack. When the sack was opened the fog flew out and hung right round the king's ships, so they could see nothing. Then they sailed back to the palace, and the king was told what strange things had happened. Meanwhile the young man's vessel reached home in safety.

'Well, here you are once more,' said the hermit. 'Now you can fulfil the promise you made me to give me the half of all you had.'

'That will I do with all my heart,' answered the youth, and began to divide all his treasures, putting part on one side for himself and setting aside the other for his friend. 'Good father, it is finished,' said he at length; 'there is nothing more left to divide.'

'Nothing more left!' cried the hermit. 'Why, you have forgotten the best thing of all!'

'What can that be?' asked the youth. 'We have divided everything.'

'And the king's daughter?' said the hermit.

Then the young man's heart stood still, for he loved her dearly. But he answered, 'It is well; I have sworn; I will keep my word,' and drew his sword to cut her in pieces.

When the hermit saw that the youth held his honor dearer than his wife, he lifted his hand and cried, 'Hold! She is yours, and all the treasures too. I gave you my help because you had pity on those who were in need. And when you are in need yourself, call upon me and I will come to you.'

As he spoke he softly touched their heads and vanished.

The next day the wedding took place, and the two brothers came to the house. They all lived happily together, but they never forgot the holy man who had been such a good friend.

[From *Silicianische Märchen*. L. Gonzenbach.]

The Sprig of Rosemary

ONCE UPON A TIME
there lived a man who had one daughter, and he made her
work hard all the day. One morning, when she had finished
everything he had set her to do, he told her to go out into the
woods and gather some dry leaves and sticks to kindle a fire.

The girl went out and soon collected a large bundle, and
then she plucked at a sprig of sweet-smelling rosemary for herself. But the harder she pulled the firmer seemed the plant. At
last, determined not to be beaten, she gave one great tug, and
the rosemary remained in her hands.

Then she heard a voice close to her saying, 'Well?' Turning
she saw before her a handsome young man, who asked why
she had come to steal his firewood.

The girl, who felt much confused, only managed to stammer
out as an excuse that her father had sent her.

'Very well,' replied the young man, 'then come with me.'

So he took her through the opening made by the torn-up root,
and they traveled till they reached a beautiful palace, splendidly
furnished, but only lighted from the top. When they had entered he told her that he was a great lord and never before had

he seen a maiden so beautiful. If she would give him her heart they would be married and live happy forever after.

The maiden said yes, she would, and so they were married.

The next day the old dame who looked after the house handed her all the keys but pointed one out to her that she would do well never to use, for if she did the whole palace would fall to the ground, the grass would grow over it, and the damsel herself would be remembered no more.

The bride promised to be careful but, in a little while, when there was nothing left for her to do, she began to wonder what could be in the chest which was opened by the key. As everybody knows, if we once begin to think we soon begin to do, and it was not very long before the key was no longer in the maiden's hand but in the lock of the chest.

But the lock was stiff and resisted all her efforts, and in the end she had to break it. And what was inside after all? Why, nothing but a serpent's skin, which her husband, who was, unknown to her, a magician, put on when he was at work. At the sight of it the girl was turning away in disgust, when the earth shook violently under her feet, the palace vanished as if it had never been, and the bride found herself in the middle of a field, not knowing where she was or whither to go.

She burst into a flood of bitter tears, partly at her own folly, but more for the loss of her husband whom she dearly loved. Then, breaking a sprig of rosemary on a bush hard by, she resolved, cost what it might, to seek him through all the world till she found him.

So she walked and she walked and she walked, till she arrived at a house built of straw. She knocked at the door and asked if they wanted a servant. The mistress said she did, and if the girl was willing she might stay. But day by day the poor maiden grew more and more sad, till at last her mistress begged her to say what was the matter. Then she told her story—how she wanted to go through all the world seeking after her husband.

And her mistress answered her, 'Where he is, none can tell better than the Sun, the Moon and the Wind, for they go everywhere!'

On hearing these words the damsel set forth once more and walked till she reached the Golden Castle where lived the Sun. And she knocked boldly at the door, saying:

'All hail, O Sun! I have come to ask if, of your charity, you will help me in my need. By my own fault have I fallen into these straits, and I am weary, for I seek my husband throughout the wide world.'

'Indeed!' spoke the Sun. 'Do you, rich as you are, need help? Though you live in a palace without windows, the Sun enters everywhere and he knows you.'

Then the bride told him the whole story and did not hide her own ill-doing. The Sun listened and was sorry for her and, though he could not tell her where to go, he gave her a nut and bade her open it in a time of great distress.

The damsel thanked him with all her heart and departed, and walked and walked and walked, till she came to another castle. She knocked at the door which was opened by an old woman.

'All hail!' said the girl. 'I have come, of your charity, to ask your help!'

'It is my mistress, the Moon, you seek. I will tell her of your prayer.'

So the Moon came out, and when she saw the maiden she knew her again, for she had watched her sleeping both in the cottage and in the palace. So she spake to her and said:

'Do you, rich as you are, need help?'

Then the girl told her the whole story, and the Moon listened and was sorry for her. Though she could not tell her where to find her husband, she gave her an almond and told her to crack it when she was in great need.

So the damsel thanked her and departed, and walked and walked and walked till she came to another castle. And she knocked at the door, and said:

'All hail! I have come to ask if, of your charity, you will help me in my need.'

'It is my lord, the Wind, that you want,' answered the old woman who opened it. 'I will tell him of your prayer.'

And the Wind looked on her and knew her again, for he had seen her in the cottage and in the palace, and he spake to her and said:

'Do you, rich as you are, want help?'

And she told him the whole story. The Wind listened and was sorry for her, and he gave her a walnut that she was to eat in time of need. But the girl did not go as the Wind expected. She was tired and sad, and knew not where to turn, so she began to weep bitterly. The Wind wept too for company, and said:

'Don't be frightened. I will go and see if I can find out something.'

And the Wind departed with a great noise and fuss, but in the twinkling of an eye, he was back again, beaming with delight.

'From what one person and another have let fall,' he exclaimed, 'I have contrived to learn that he is in the palace of the king, who keeps him hidden lest anyone should see him! To-morrow he is to marry the princess who, ill-tempered creature that she is, has not been able to find any man to wed her.'

Who can tell the despair which seized the poor maiden when

she heard this news! As soon as she could speak she implored the Wind to do all he could to get the wedding put off for two or three days, for it would take her all that time to reach the palace of the king.

The Wind gladly promised to do what he could and, as he traveled much faster than the maiden, he soon arrived at the palace, where he found five tailors working night and day on the wedding clothes of the princess.

Down came the Wind right in the middle of their lace and satin and trimmings of pearl! Away they all went whiz! through the open windows, right up into the tops of the trees across the river, among the dancing ears of corn! After them ran the tailors, catching, jumping, climbing, but all to no purpose! The lace was torn, the satin stained, the pearls knocked off! There was nothing for it but to go to the shops to buy fresh and to begin all over again! It was plainly quite impossible that the wedding clothes could be ready next day.

However, the king was much too anxious to see his daughter married to listen to any excuses, and he declared that a dress must be put together somehow for the bride to wear. But when he went to look at the princess, she made such a poor figure that he agreed it would be unfitting for her position to be seen in such a gown, and he ordered the ceremony and the banquet to be postponed for a few hours that the tailors might take the dress to pieces and make it fit.

But by this time the maiden had arrived, footsore and weary, at the castle. As soon as she reached the door she cracked her nut and drew out of it the most beautiful mantle in the world. Then she rang the bell, and asked:

'Is not the princess to be married today?'

'Yes, she is.'

'Ask her if she would like to buy this mantle.'

When the princess saw the mantle she was delighted, for her wedding mantle had been spoilt with all the other things and it was too late to make another. So she told the maiden to ask what price she would and it should be given her.

The maiden fixed a large sum, many pieces of gold, but the princess had set her heart on the mantle and gave it readily.

Now the maiden hid her gold in the pocket of her dress and turned away from the castle. The moment she was out of sight she broke her almond and drew from it the most magnificent petticoats that ever were seen. Then she went back to the castle and asked if the princess wished to buy any petticoats.

No sooner did the princess cast her eyes on them than she declared they were even more beautiful than the mantle, and that she would give the maiden whatever price she wanted for the petticoats. And the maiden named many pieces of gold which the princess paid her gladly, so pleased was she with her new possessions.

Then the girl went down the steps where none could watch her and cracked her walnut, and out came the most splendid court dress that any dressmaker had ever invented. Carrying it carefully in her arms, she knocked at the door and asked if the princess wished to buy a court dress.

When the message was delivered the princess sprang to her feet with delight, for she had been thinking that, after all, it was not much use to have a lovely mantle and elegant petticoats if she had no dress, and she knew the tailors would never be ready in time. So she sent at once to say she would buy the dress, and what sum did the maiden want for it?

This time the maiden answered that the price of the dress was the permission to see the bridegroom.

The princess was not at all pleased when she heard the maiden's reply but, as she could not do without the dress, she was forced to give in and contented herself with thinking that, after all, it did not matter much.

So the maiden was led to the rooms which had been given to her husband. And when she came near she touched him with the sprig of rosemary that she carried. His memory came back, and he knew her, and kissed her, and declared that she was his true wife, and that he loved her and no other.

Then they went back to the maiden's home where they grew to be very old, and lived happy all the days of their life.

[From *Cuentos Populars Catalans,* by D. Francisco de S. Maspons y Labros. Barcelona, 1885.]

The Golden Lion

Here was once a rich
merchant who had three sons, and when they were grown
up the eldest said to him, 'Father, I wish to travel and see the
world. I pray you let me.'

So the father ordered a beautiful ship to be fitted up, and the
young man sailed away in it. After some weeks the vessel cast
anchor before a large town, and the merchant's son went on
shore.

The first thing he saw was a large notice written on a board,
saying that if any man could find the king's daughter within
eight days he should have her to wife, but that if he tried and
failed his head must be the forfeit.

Well, thought the youth, as he read this proclamation, that
should not be a very difficult matter. So he asked an audience of
the king, and told him that he wished to seek for the princess.

'Certainly,' replied the king. 'You have the whole palace to
search in; but remember, if you fail it will cost you your head.'

So saying, he commanded the doors to be thrown open, and
food and drink to be set before the young man who, after he
had eaten, began to look for the princess. But though he visited
every corner and chest and cupboard, she was not in any of

them, and after eight days he gave it up and his head was cut off.

All this time his father and brothers had heard no news of him and were very anxious. At last the second son could bear it no longer, and said:

'Dear father, give me, I pray you, a large ship and some money, and let me go and seek for my brother.'

So another ship was fitted out, and the young man sailed away and was blown by the wind into the same harbor where his brother had landed.

Now when he saw the first ship lying at anchor, his heart beat high, and he said to himself, 'My brother surely cannot be far off.' And he ordered a boat and was put on shore.

As he jumped on to the pier his eye caught the notice about the princess, and he said, 'He has undertaken to find her and has certainly lost his head. I must try myself and seek him as well as her. It cannot be such a very difficult matter.' But he fared no better than his brother, and in eight days his head was cut off.

So now there was only the youngest at home and, when the other two failed to return, he also begged for a ship that he might go in search of his lost brothers. When the vessel started, a high wind arose and blew him straight to the harbor where the notice was set.

'Oho,' said he, as he read, 'whoever can find the king's daughter shall have her to wife. It is quite clear now what has befallen my brothers. But, in spite of that, I think I must try my luck.'

And he took the road to the castle. On the way he met an old woman, who stopped him and begged.

'Leave me in peace, old woman,' replied he.

'Oh, do not send me away empty,' she said. 'You are such a

handsome young man surely you will not refuse an old woman a few pence.'

'I tell you, old woman, leave me alone.'

'You are in some trouble?' she asked. 'Tell me what it is and perhaps I can help you.'

Then he told her how he had set his heart on finding the king's daughter.

'I can easily manage that for you as long as you have enough gold.'

'Oh, as to that, I have plenty,' answered he.

'Well, you must take it to a goldsmith and have him make it into a golden lion, with eyes of crystal. Inside it must have something that will enable it to play tunes. When it is ready bring it to me.'

The young man did as he was told, and when the lion was made, the old woman hid the youth in it and brought it to the king who was so delighted with it that he wanted to buy it.

But she replied, 'It does not belong to me, and my master will not part with it at any price.'

'At any rate, leave it with me for a few days,' said the king, 'I should like to show it to my daughter.'

'Yes, I can do that,' answered the old woman, 'but tomorrow I must have it back again.' And she went away.

The king watched her till she was quite out of sight, so as to make sure that she was not spying upon him, then he took the golden lion into his room and lifted some loose boards from the floor. Below the floor there was a staircase, which he went down till he reached a door at the foot. This he unlocked and found himself in a narrow passage closed by another door, which he also opened.

The young man, hidden in the golden lion, kept count of everything and marked that there were in all seven doors. After

they had all been unlocked the king entered a lovely hall where the princess was amusing herself with eleven friends. All twelve girls wore the same clothes and were as like each other as two peas.

'What bad luck!' the youth said to himself. 'Even supposing that I managed to find my way here again, I don't see how I could ever tell which was the princess.'

And he stared hard at the princess as she clapped her hands with joy and ran up to them, crying, 'Oh, do let us keep that splendid beast for tonight. It will make such a nice plaything.'

The king did not stay long, and when he left he handed over the lion to the maidens, who amused themselves with it for some time, till they grew sleepy and thought it was time to go to bed. But the princess took the lion into her own room and set it on the floor.

She was just beginning to doze when she heard a voice quite close to her, which made her jump.

'O lovely Princess, if you only knew what I have gone through to find you!'

The princess jumped out of bed screaming, 'The lion! The lion!' But her friends thought it was a nightmare and did not trouble themselves to get up.

'O lovely Princess,' continued the voice, 'fear nothing! I am the son of a rich merchant and desire above all things to have you for my wife. And in order to get to you I have hidden myself in this golden lion.'

'What use is that?' she asked. 'For if you cannot pick me out from among my companions you will still lose your head.'

'I look to you to help me,' he said. 'I have done so much for you that you might do this one thing for me.'

'Then listen to me. On the eighth day I will tie a white sash round my waist and by that you will know me.'

The next morning the king came very early to fetch the lion as the old woman was already at the palace asking for it. When they were safe from view she let the young man out, and he returned to the king and told him that he wished to find the princess.

'Very good,' said the king, who by this time was almost tired of repeating the same words, 'but if you fail your head will be the forfeit.'

So the youth quietly remained in the castle, eating and looking at all the beautiful things around him and, every now and then, pretending to be searching busily in all the closets and corners. On the eighth day he entered the room where the king was sitting.

'Take up the floor in this place,' he said.

The king gave a cry, but stopped himself, and asked, 'What do you want the floor up for? There is nothing there.'

But as all his courtiers were watching him he did not like to make any more objections and ordered the floor to be taken up as the young man desired. The youth then went straight down the staircase till he reached the door. Then he turned and demanded that the key should be brought. So the king was forced to unlock the door and the next and the next and the next, till all seven were open, and they entered into the hall where the twelve maidens were standing all in a row, so like that none might tell them apart.

But as the youth looked one of them silently drew a white sash from her pocket and slipped it round her waist, and the young man sprang to her, and said, 'This is the princess and I claim her for my wife.' Then the king owned himself beaten and commanded that the wedding feast should be held.

After eight days the bridal pair said farewell to the king and set sail for the youth's own country, taking with them a whole shipload of treasures as the princess' dowry. But they did not forget the old woman who had brought about all their happiness and they gave her enough money to make her comfortable to the end of her days.

[From *Sicilianische Märchen*. L. Gonzenbach.]

The Water of Life

THREE BROTHERS AND one sister lived together in a small cottage, and they loved one another dearly. One day the eldest brother, who had never done anything but amuse himself from sunrise to sunset, said to the rest, 'Let us all work hard and perhaps we shall grow rich and be able to build ourselves a palace.'

And his brothers and sister answered joyfully, 'Yes, we will all work!'

So they fell to working with all their might, till at last they became rich, and were able to build themselves a beautiful palace; and everyone came from miles round to see its wonders and to say how splendid it was. No one thought of finding any faults, till at length an old woman, who had been walking through the rooms with a crowd of people, suddenly exclaimed:

'Yes, it is a splendid palace, but there is still something it needs!'

'And what may that be?'

'A church.'

When they heard this the brothers set to work again to earn some more money, and when they had enough they set about building a church, which should be as large and beautiful as the palace itself.

And after the church was finished greater numbers of people than ever flocked to see the palace and the church and vast gardens and magnificent halls.

But one day, as the brothers were as usual doing the honors to their guests, an old man turned to them and said:

'Yes, it is all most beautiful, but there is still something it needs.'

'And what may that be?'

'A pitcher of the water of life, a branch of the tree, the smell of whose flowers gives eternal beauty, and the talking bird.'

'And where am I to find all those?'

'Go to the mountain that is far off yonder and you will find what you seek.'

After the old man had bowed politely and taken farewell of them, the eldest brother said to the rest, 'I will go in search of the water of life and the talking bird and the tree of beauty.'

'But suppose some evil befalls you?' asked his sister. 'How shall we know?'

'You are right,' he replied. 'I had not thought of that!'

Then the brothers followed the old man, and said to him, 'Our eldest brother wishes to seek for the water of life and the tree of beauty and the talking bird that you tell him are needful to make our palace perfect. But how shall we know if any evil thing befall him?'

So the old man took out a knife and gave it to them, saying, 'Keep this carefully, and as long as the blade is bright all is well. But if the blade is stained, then know that evil has befallen him.'

The brothers thanked him, and departed, and went straight to the palace, where they found the young man making ready to set out for the mountain where the treasures he longed for lay hidden.

And he walked and he walked and he walked, till he had gone a great way, and there he met a giant.

'Can you tell me how much farther I have still to go before I reach that mountain yonder?'

'And why do you wish to go there?'

'I am seeking the water of life, the talking bird and a branch of the tree of beauty.'

'Many have passed by, seeking those treasures, but none have ever come back; and you will never come back either, unless you mark my words. Follow this path, and when you reach the mountain you will find it covered with stones. Do not stop to look at them, but keep on your way. As you go you will hear scoffs and laughter behind you; and it will be the stones that mock. Do not heed them; above all, do not turn round. If you do you will become as one of them. Walk straight on till you reach the top, and then take all you wish for.'

The young man thanked him for his counsel, and walked and walked and walked, till he reached the mountain. And as he climbed he heard behind him scoffs and jeers, but he kept his ears steadily closed to them. At last the noise grew so loud that he lost patience and stooped to pick up a stone to hurl into the midst of the clamor, when suddenly his arm seemed to stiffen, and the next moment he was a stone himself!

That day his sister, who thought her brother's steps were long in returning, took out the knife and found the blade was red as blood. Then she cried out to her brothers that something terrible had come to pass.

'I will go and find him,' said the second. And he went.

He walked and he walked and he walked, till he met the

giant, and asked him if he had seen a young man traveling toward the mountain.

And the giant answered, 'Yes, I have seen him pass, but I have not seen him come back. The spell must have worked upon him.'

'Then what can I do to disenchant him, and find the water of life, the talking bird and a branch of the tree of beauty?'

'Follow this path, and when you reach the mountain you will find it covered with stones. Do not stop to look at them, but climb steadily on. Above all, heed not the laughter and scoffs that will arise on all sides, and never turn round. And when you reach the top you can then take all you desire.'

The young man thanked him for his counsel and set out for the mountain. But no sooner did he reach it than loud jests and gibes broke out on every side and almost deafened him. For some time he let them rail and pushed boldly on till he had passed the place which his brother had gained; then suddenly he thought that among the scoffing sounds he heard his brother's voice. He stopped and looked back; and another stone was added to the number.

Meanwhile the sister left at home was counting the days when her two brothers should return to her. The time seemed long, and it would be hard to say how often she took out the knife and looked at its polished blade to make sure that this second brother at least was still safe. The blade was always bright and clear; each time she looked at it she had the happiness of knowing that all was well.

But one evening, tired and anxious, as she frequently was at the end of the day, she took it from its drawer, and behold! The blade was red as blood. Her cry of horror brought her youngest brother to her and, unable to speak, she held out the knife!

'I will go,' he said.

So he walked and he walked and he walked till he met the giant, and he asked, 'Have two young men, making for yonder mountain, passed this way?'

And the giant answered, 'Yes, they have passed by, but they never came back, and by this I know that the spell has fallen upon them.'

'Then what must I do to free them and to get the water of life and the talking bird and the branch of the tree of beauty?'

'Go to the mountain, which you will find so thickly covered with stones that you will hardly be able to place your feet, and walk straight forward, turning neither to the right hand nor to the left, and paying no heed to the laughter and scoffs which will follow you, till you reach the top, and then you may take all that you desire.'

The young man thanked the giant for his counsel and set forth to the mountain. And when he began to climb there burst forth all around him a storm of scoffs and jeers; but he thought of the giant's words and looked neither to the right hand nor to the left, till the mountain top lay straight before him. A moment now and he would have gained it, when, through the groans and yells, he heard his brothers' voices. He turned, and there was one stone the more.

All this while his sister was pacing up and down the palace, hardly letting the knife out of her hand, and dreading what she knew she would see, and what she did see. The blade grew red before her eyes, and she said, 'Now it is my turn.'

So she walked and she walked and she walked till she came to the giant, and prayed him to tell her if he had seen three young men pass that way seeking the distant mountain.

'I have seen them pass, but they have never returned, and by this I know that the spell has fallen upon them.'

'And what must I do to set them free and to find the water

of life and the talking bird and a branch of the tree of beauty?'

'You must go to that mountain, which is so full of stones that your feet will hardly find a place to tread, and as you climb you will hear a noise as if all the stones in the world were mocking you. But pay no heed to anything you may hear and, once you gain the top, you have gained everything.'

The girl thanked him for the counsel, and set out for the mountain; and scarcely had she gone a few steps upward when cries and screams broke forth round her, and she felt as if each stone she trod on was a living thing. But she remembered the words of the giant, and knew not what had befallen her brothers, and kept her face steadily toward the mountaintop, which grew nearer and nearer every moment. As she mounted the clamor increased sevenfold: high above them all rang the voices of her three brothers. But the girl took no heed, and at last her feet stood upon the top.

Then she looked round and saw, lying in a hollow, the pool of the water of life. And she took the brazen pitcher that she had brought with her and filled it to the brim. By the side of the pool stood the tree of beauty, with the talking bird on one of its boughs; and she caught the bird and placed it in a cage, and broke off one of the branches.

After that she turned and went joyfully down the mountain again, carrying her treasures, but her long climb had tired her out, and the brazen pitcher was very heavy. As she walked a few drops of the water spilt on the stones, and as it touched them they changed into young men and maidens, crowding about her to give thanks for their deliverance.

So she learned by this how the evil spell might be broken, and she carefully sprinkled every stone till there was not one left— only a great company of youths and girls who followed her down the mountain.

When they arrived at the palace she did not lose a moment in planting the branch of the tree of beauty and watering it with the water of life. And the branch shot up into a tree, and was heavy with flowers, and the talking bird nestled in its branches.

Now the fame of these wonders was noised abroad, and the people flocked in great numbers to see the three marvels and the maiden who had won them. Among the sightseers came the king's son, who would not go till everything was shown him and he had heard how it had all happened.

The prince admired the strangeness and beauty of the treasures in the palace, but more than all he admired the beauty and courage of the maiden who had brought them there. So he went home and told his parents, and gained their consent to wed her for his wife.

The marriage was celebrated in the church adjoining the palace. Then the bridegroom took her to his own home, where they lived happy for ever after.

[From *Cuentos Populars Catalans*, by D. Francisco de S. Maspons y Labros. Barcelona, 1885.]

A Lost Paradise

IN THE MIDDLE OF A GREAT forest there lived a long time ago a charcoal burner and his wife. They were both young and handsome and strong and, when they had married, they thought work would never fail them. But bad times came, and they grew poorer and poorer, and the nights in which they went hungry to bed became more and more frequent.

Now, one evening, the king of that country was hunting near the charcoal-burner's hut. As he passed the door he heard a sound of sobbing, and being a good-hearted man he stopped to listen, thinking that perhaps he might be able to give some help.

'Were there ever two people so unhappy?' said a woman's voice. 'Here we are, ready to work like slaves the whole day long and no work can we get. And it is all because of the curiosity of old mother Eve! If she had only been like me, who never wants to know anything, we should all have been as happy as kings today, with plenty to eat and warm clothes to wear. Why—'

But at this point a loud knock interrupted her lamentations.

'Who is there?' asked she.

'I!' replied somebody.

'And who is "I"?'

'The king. Let me in.'

Full of surprise the woman pulled the bar away from the door. As the king entered, he noticed there was no furniture in the room at all, not even a chair, so he pretended to be in too great a hurry to see anything around him, and only said:

'You must not let me disturb you, I have no time to stay, but you seemed to be in trouble. Tell me, are you very unhappy?'

'Oh, my lord, we can find no work and have eaten nothing for two days!' answered she. 'Nothing remains for us but to die of hunger.'

'No, no, you shall not do that!' cried the king. 'If you do, it will be your own fault. You shall come with me to my palace and you will feel as if you were in Paradise, I promise you. In return, I only ask one thing of you, that you shall obey my orders exactly.'

The charcoal burner and his wife both stared at him for a moment, as if they could hardly believe their ears; and, indeed, it was not to be wondered at. Then they found their tongues, and exclaimed together:

'Oh, yes, yes, my lord! We will do everything you tell us. How could we be so ungrateful as to disobey you, when you are so kind?'

The king smiled, and his eyes twinkled.

'Well, let us start at once,' said he. 'Lock your door and put the key in your pocket.'

The woman looked as if she thought this was needless, seeing it was quite, quite certain they would never come back. But she dared not say so and did as the king told her.

After walking through the forest for a couple of miles, they all three reached the palace, and by the king's orders servants led the charcoal burner and his wife into rooms filled with beautiful things such as they had never even dreamed of. First they bathed in green-marble baths where the water looked like the sea, and then they put on silken clothes that felt soft and pleasant. When they were ready, one of the king's special servants entered and took them into a small hall, where dinner was laid, and this pleased them better than anything else.

They were just about to sit down to the table when the king walked in.

'I hope you have been attended to properly,' said he, 'and that you will enjoy your dinner. My steward will take care you have all you want, and I wish you to do exactly as you please. Oh, by the by, there is one thing! You notice that soup tureen in the middle of the table? Well, be careful on no account to lift the lid. If once you take off the cover, there is an end of your good fortune.'

Then, bowing to his guests, he left the room.

'Did you hear what he said?' inquired the charcoal burner in an awe-stricken voice. 'We are to have what we want, and do what we please. Only we must not touch the soup tureen.'

'No, of course we won't,' answered the wife. 'Why should we wish to? But all the same it is rather odd, and one can't help wondering what is inside.'

For many days life went on like a beautiful dream to the charcoal burner and his wife. Their beds were so comfortable they could hardly make up their minds to get up; their clothes were so lovely they could scarcely bring themselves to take them off; their dinners were so good they found it very difficult to leave off eating. Then outside the palace were gardens filled with rare flowers and fruits and singing birds, or if they desired to go farther, a golden coach, painted with wreaths of forget-me-nots, and lined with blue satin, awaited their orders.

Sometimes it happened that the king came to see them, and he smiled as he glanced at the man who was growing rosier and plumper each day. But when his eyes rested on the woman, they took on a look which seemed to say 'I knew it,' though this neither the charcoal burner nor his wife ever noticed.

'Why are you so silent?' asked the man one day, when dinner had passed before his wife had uttered one word. 'A little while ago you used to be chattering all the day long. Now I have almost forgotten the sound of your voice.'

'Oh, nothing; I did not feel inclined to talk, that was all!' She stopped, and added carelessly after a pause, 'Don't you ever wonder what is in that soup tureen?'

'No, never,' replied the man. 'It is no affair of ours,' and the conversation dropped once more. But as time went on, the woman spoke less and less and seemed so wretched that her husband grew quite frightened about her. As to her food, she refused one thing after another.

'My dear wife,' said the man at last, 'you really must eat something. What in the world is the matter with you? If you go on like this you will die.'

'I would rather die than not know what is in that tureen,' she burst forth so violently that her husband was quite startled.

'Is that it?' cried he. 'Are you making yourself miserable because of that? Why, you know we should be turned out of the palace and sent away to starve.'

'Oh no, we shouldn't. The king is too good-natured. Of course he didn't mean a little thing like this! Besides, there is no need to lift the lid off altogether. Just raise one corner so I may peep. We are quite alone. Nobody will ever know.'

The man hesitated. It did seem a little thing, and if it was to

make his wife contented and happy it was well worth the risk. So he took hold of the handle of the cover and raised it very slowly and carefully, while the woman stooped down to peep. Suddenly she started back with a scream, for a small mouse had sprung from the inside of the tureen, and had nearly hit her in the eye.

Round and round the room it ran, round and round they both ran after it, knocking down chairs and vases in their efforts to catch the mouse and put it back in the tureen. In the midst of all the noise the door opened, and the mouse ran out between the feet of the king. In one instant both the man and his wife were hiding under the table, and to all appearance the room was empty.

'You may as well come out,' said the king, 'and hear what I have to say.'

'I know what it is,' answered the charcoal burner, hanging his head. 'The mouse has escaped.'

'A guard of soldiers will take you back to your hut,' said the king. 'Your wife has the key.'

'WEREN'T they silly?' cried the grandchildren of the charcoal burners when they heard the story. 'How we wish that we had had the chance! We should never have wanted to know what was in the soup tureen!'

[From *Littérature Orale de l'Auvergne*, by P. Sebillot.]

The False Prince and the True

THE KING HAD JUST awakened from his midday sleep, for it was summer, and everyone rose early and then rested from twelve to three, as they do in hot countries. He had dressed himself in cool white clothes and was passing through the hall on his way to the council chamber, when a number of young nobles suddenly appeared before him, and one amongst them stepped forward and spoke.

'Sire, this morning we were all playing tennis in the court, the prince and this gentleman with the rest, when there broke out some dispute about the game. The prince lost his temper and said many insulting things to the other, who was playing against him, till at length the gentleman whom you see there struck him violently in the face.

'We were all so horrified at the sight that we should most likely have killed the man then and there, for daring to lay hands on the prince, had not his grandfather the duke stepped between them and commanded us to lay the affair before you.'

The king had listened attentively to the story, and when it was ended he said, 'I suppose the prince had no arms with him, or else he would have used them?'

'Yes, sire, he had arms; he always carries a dagger in his belt.

But when he saw the blood pouring from his face, he went to a corner of the court and began to cry, which was the strangest thing of all.'

On hearing this the king walked to the window and stood for a few minutes with his back to the room, where the company of young men remained silent. Then he came back, his face white and stern.

'I tell you,' he said, 'and it is the solemn truth, that I would rather you had told me the prince was dead, though he is my only son, than know he would suffer such an injury without attempting to avenge it. As for the gentleman, who struck him, he will be brought before my judges and will plead his own cause, but I hardly think he can escape death, after having assaulted the heir to the crown.'

The young man raised his head as if to reply, but the king would not listen and commanded his guards to put him under arrest, adding, however, that if the prisoner wished to visit any part of the city, he was at liberty to do so properly guarded, and in fifteen days he would be brought to trial before the highest judges in the land.

The young man left the king's presence, surrounded by soldiers, and accompanied by many of his friends, for he was a great favorite. By their advice he spent the fourteen days that remained to him going about to seek counsel from wise men of all sorts as to how he might escape death, but no one could help him, for none could find any excuse for the blow he had given to the prince.

The fourteenth night had come, and in despair the prisoner went out to take his last walk through the city. He wandered on, hardly knowing where he went, and his face was so white and desperate that none of his companions dared speak to him.

The sad little procession had passed some hours in this manner when, near the gate of a monastery, an old woman appeared round a corner, and suddenly stood before the young man. She was bent almost double, and was so wizened and wrinkled that she looked at least ninety; only her eyes were bright and quick as those of a girl.

'Sir,' she said, 'I know all that has happened to you, and how you are seeking if in any wise you can save your life. But there is none who can answer that question save only I, myself, if you will promise to do all I ask.'

At her words the prisoner felt as if a load had all at once been rolled off him.

'Oh, save me, and I will do anything!' he cried. 'It is so hard to leave the world and go out into the darkness.'

'You will not need to do that,' answered the old woman. 'You have only to marry me, and you will soon be free.'

'Marry you?' exclaimed he. 'But—but—I am not yet twenty, and you—why, you must be a hundred at least! Oh, no, it is quite impossible!'

He spoke without thinking, but the flash of anger which darted from her eyes made him feel uncomfortable. However, all she said was:

'As you like; since you reject me, let the crows have you.' And she hurried away down the street.

Left to himself, the full horror of his coming death rushed upon the young man, and he understood that he had thrown away his sole chance of life. Well, if he must, he must, he said to himself, and began to run as fast as he could after the old crone who by this time could scarcely be seen, even in the moonlight. Who would have believed a woman past ninety could walk with such speed? It seemed more like flying! But at length, breathless and exhausted, he reached her side, and gasped out:

'Madam, pardon me for my hasty words just now. I was wrong and will thankfully accept the offer you made me.'

'Ah, I thought you would come to your senses,' answered she, in rather an odd voice. 'We have no time to lose—follow me at once.' And they went on silently and swiftly till they stopped at the door of a small house in which the priest lived. Before him the old woman bade the prisoner swear that she should be his wife, and this he did in the presence of witnesses. Then, begging the priest and the guards to leave them alone for a little, she told the young man what he was to do, when the next morning he was brought before the king and the judges.

THE hall was full to overflowing when the prisoner entered it, and all marveled at the brightness of his face. The king inquired if he had any excuse to plead for the high treason he had committed by striking the heir to the throne and, if so, to be quick in setting it forth. With a low bow the youth made answer in a clear voice:

'O my lord and gracious King, and you, nobles and wise men of the land, I leave my cause without fear in your hands, knowing that you will listen and judge rightly, and that you will suffer me to speak to the end, before you give judgment.

'For four years you, O King, had been married to the queen and yet had no children, which grieved you greatly. The queen saw this, and likewise that your love was going from her, and thought night and day of some plan that might put an end to this evil. At length, when you were away fighting in distant countries, she decided what she would do and adopted in secret the baby of a poor quarryman, sending a messenger to tell you that you had a son. No one suspected the truth except a priest to whom the queen confessed the truth, and in a few weeks she fell ill and died, leaving the baby to be brought up as became a prince. And now, if Your Highness will permit me, I will speak of myself.'

'What you have already told me,' answered the king, 'is so strange that I cannot imagine what more there is to tell, but go on with your story.'

'One day, shortly after the death of the queen,' continued the young man, 'Your Highness was hunting and outstripped all your attendants while chasing the deer. You were in a part of the country which you did not know, so seeing an orchard all pink and white with apple blossoms, and a girl tossing a ball in one corner, you went up to her to ask your way.

'But when she turned to answer you, you were so struck with her beauty that all else fled from your mind. Again and again you rode back to see her, and at length persuaded her to marry you. She thought you only a poor knight and agreed that, as you wished it, the marriage should be kept secret.

'After the ceremony you gave her three rings and a charm with a cross on it, and then put her in a cottage in the forest, thinking to hide the matter securely.

'For some months you visited the cottage every week, but a rebellion broke out in a distant part of the kingdom and called for your presence. When next you rode up to the cottage, it was empty, and none could inform you whither your bride had gone. That, sire, I can now tell you.' The young man paused and looked at the king, who colored deeply.

'She went back to her father the old duke, once your chamberlain, and the cross on her breast revealed at once who you were. Fierce was his anger when he heard his daughter's tale, and he vowed that he would hide her safely from you till the day came when you would claim her publicly as your queen.

'By-and-by I was born and was brought up by my grandfather in one of his great houses. Here are the rings you gave to my mother, and here is the cross. These will prove if I am your son or not.'

As he spoke the young man laid the jewels at the feet of the king, and the nobles and the judges pressed round to examine them. The king alone did not move from his seat, for he had forgotten the hall of justice and all about him, and saw only the apple orchard as it was twenty years ago and the beautiful girl playing at ball. A sudden silence round him made him look up, and he found the eyes of the assembly fixed on him.

'It is true; it is he who is my son, and not the other,' he said with an effort. 'And let every man present swear to acknowledge him as king, after my death.'

Therefore, one by one, they all knelt before him and took the oath, and a message was sent to the false prince, telling him what had happened and that a handsome pension was granted him.

At last the ceremony was over and the king, signing to his newly found son to follow him, rose and went into another room.

'Tell me how you knew all that,' he said, throwing himself into a carved chair filled with crimson cushions.

Then the prince told of his meeting with the old woman who had brought him the jewels from his mother, and how he had sworn before a priest to marry her, though he did not want to do it, on account of the difference in their ages, and besides, he would rather receive a bride chosen by the king himself. But the king frowned, and answered sharply:

'You swore to marry her if she save your life and, come what may, you must fulfil your promise.' Then, striking a silver shield that hung close by, he said to the equerry who appeared immediately:

'Go and seek the priest, who lives near the door of the prison, and ask him where you can find the old woman who visited him last night. When you have found her, bring her to the palace.'

IT took some time to discover the whereabouts of the old woman, but at length it was accomplished and, when she arrived at the palace with the equerry, she was received with royal honors, as became the bride of the prince. The guards looked at each other with astonished eyes as the wizened creature, bowed with age, passed between their lines; but they were more amazed still at the lightness of her step as she skipped up the steps to the great door before which the king was standing, with the prince at his side. If they both felt a shock at the appearance of the aged lady they did not show it, and the king, with a grave bow, took her hand and led her to the chapel, where a bishop was waiting to perform the marriage ceremony.

For the next few weeks little was seen of the prince, who spent all his days in hunting and trying to forget the old wife at home. As for the princess, no one troubled himself about her, and she passed the days alone in her apartments, for she had absolutely declined the services of the ladies-in-waiting whom the king had appointed for her.

One night the prince returned after a longer chase than usual, and he was so tired that he went up straight to bed. Suddenly he was awakened by a strange noise in the room, and suspecting that a robber might have stolen in, he jumped out of bed and seized his sword, which lay ready to his hand. Then he perceived that the noise proceeded from the next room, which belonged to the princess, and was lighted by a burning torch.

Creeping softly to the door, he peeped through it and beheld her lying quietly, with a crown of gold and pearls upon her head, her wrinkles all gone, and her face, which was whiter than the snow, as fresh as that of a girl of fourteen. Could that really be his wife—that beautiful, beautiful creature?

The prince was still gazing in surprise when the lady opened her eyes and smiled at him.

'Yes, I really am your wife,' she said, as if she had guessed his thoughts, 'and the enchantment is ended. Now I must tell you who I am, and what befell to cause me to take the shape of an old woman.

'The King of Granada is my father, and I was born in the palace which overlooks the plain of the Vega. I was only a few months old when a wicked fairy, who had a spite against my parents, cast a spell over me, bending my back and wrinkling my skin till I looked as if I was a hundred years old, and making me such an object of disgust to everyone, that at length the king ordered my nurse to take me away from the palace. She was the only person who cared about me, and we lived together in this city on a small pension allowed me by the king.

'When I was about three an old man arrived at our house and begged my nurse to let him come in and rest, as he could walk no longer. She saw that he was very ill so she put him to bed and took such care of him that, by-and-by, he was as strong as ever.

'In gratitude for her goodness to him, he told her that he was a wizard and could give her anything she chose to ask for, except life or death, so she answered that what she longed for most in the world was that my wrinkled skin should disappear and that I should regain the beauty with which I was born. To this he replied that as my misfortune resulted from a spell, this was rather difficult, but he would do his best, and at any rate he could promise that before my fifteenth birthday I should be freed from the enchantment if I could get a man who would swear to marry me as I was.

'As you may suppose this was not easy, as my ugliness was such that no one would look at me a second time. My nurse and I were almost in despair, as my fifteenth birthday was drawing near, and I had never so much as spoken to a man. At last we received a visit from the wizard, who told us what had happened at court and your story, bidding me to put myself in your way, when you had lost all hope, and offer to save you if you would consent to marry me.

'That is my history, and now you must beg the king to send messengers at once to Granada, to inform my father of our marriage, and I think,' she added with a smile, 'that he will not refuse us his blessing.'

[From the Portuguese.]

The Castle of Kerglas

PERONNIK WAS A POOR foolish boy who belonged to nobody, and he would have died of starvation if it had not been for the kindness of the village people, who gave him food whenever he chose to ask for it. As for a bed, when night came and he grew sleepy, he looked about for a heap of straw and, making a hole in it, crept in like a lizard. He was never unhappy, but always thanked gratefully those who fed him, and sometimes he would stop for a little and sing to them. For he could imitate a lark so well that no one knew which was Peronnik and which was the bird.

He had been wandering in a forest one day for several hours, and when evening approached he suddenly felt very hungry. Luckily, just at that place the trees grew thinner, and he could see a small farmhouse a little way off. Peronnik went straight toward it and found the farmer's wife standing at the door, holding in her hands the large bowl out of which her children had eaten their supper.

'I am hungry, will you give me something to eat?' asked the boy.

'If you can find anything here, you are welcome to it,' an-swered she. And, indeed, there was not much left as everybody's spoon had dipped in. But Peronnik ate what was there with a hearty appetite and thought that he had never tasted better food.

'It is made of the finest flour and mixed with the richest milk and stirred by the best cook in all the countryside,' and though he said it to himself, the woman heard him.

'Poor innocent,' she murmured, 'he does not know what he is saying, but I will cut him a slice of that new wheaten loaf.' So she did, and Peronnik ate up every crumb and declared that nobody less than the bishop's baker could have baked it. This flattered the farmer's wife so much that she gave him some butter to spread on a new piece. Peronnik was eating it on the doorstep when an armed knight rode up.

'Can you tell me the way to the castle of Kerglas?' asked he.

'To Kerglas? Are you really going to Kerglas?' cried the woman, turning pale.

'Yes, and in order to get there I have come from a country so far off that it has taken me three months' hard riding to travel as far as this.'

'And why do you want to go to Kerglas?' asked she.

' I am seeking the basin of gold and the lance of diamonds which are in the castle,' he answered.

Then Peronnik looked up. 'The basin and the lance are very costly things,' he said suddenly.

'More costly and precious than all the crowns in the world,' replied the stranger, 'for not only will the basin furnish you with the best food that you can dream of, but if you drink of it, it will cure you of any illness, however dangerous, and will even bring the dead back to life, if it touches their mouths. As to the diamond lance, that will cut through any stone or metal.'

'And to whom do these wonders belong?' asked Peronnik in amazement.

'To a magician named Rogéar, who lives in the castle,' answered the woman. 'Every day he passes along here, mounted on a black mare, with a colt thirteen months old trotting behind. But no one dares to attack him, as he always carries his lance.'

'That is true,' said the knight, 'but there is a spell laid upon him which forbids his using it within the castle of Kerglas. The moment he enters, the basin and lance are put away in a dark cellar which no key but one can open. And that is the place where I wish to fight the magician.'

'You will never overcome him, Sir Knight,' replied the woman, shaking her head. 'More than a hundred gentlemen have ridden past this house bent on the same errand, and not one has ever come back.'

'I know that, good woman,' returned the knight, 'but then they did not have, like me, instructions from the hermit of Blavet.'

'And what did the hermit tell you?' asked Peronnik.

'He told me that I should have to pass through a wood full of all sorts of enchantments and voices, which would try to frighten me and make me lose my way. Most of those who have gone before me have wandered they know not where, and perished from cold, hunger, or fatigue.'

'Well, suppose you get through safely?' asked Peronnik.

'If I do,' continued the knight, 'I shall then meet a sort of fairy armed with a needle of fire which burns to ashes all it touches. This dwarf stands guarding an apple tree, from which I am bound to pluck an apple.'

'And next?' inquired Peronnik.

'Next I shall find the flower that laughs, protected by a lion whose mane is formed of vipers. I must pluck that flower and go on to the lake of the dragons and fight the black man who holds in his hand the iron ball, which never misses its mark and returns of its own accord to its master. After that, I enter the valley of pleasure, where some who conquered all the other obstacles have left their bones. If I can win through this, I shall reach a river with only one ford, where a lady in black will be seated. She will mount my horse behind me and tell me what I am to do next.'

He paused, and the woman shook her head.

'You will never be able to do all that,' said she. But the knight bade her remember these were matters only for men, and he galloped away down the path she pointed out.

The farmer's wife sighed and, giving Peronnik some more food, bade him good night. The boy rose and was opening the gate which led into the forest when the farmer himself came up.

'I want a boy to tend my cattle,' he said abruptly, 'as the one I had has run away. Will you stay and do it?'

Peronnik, though he loved his liberty and hated work, recollected the good food he had eaten and agreed to stop.

At sunrise he collected his herd carefully and led them to the rich pasture which lay along the borders of the forest, cutting himself a hazel wand with which to keep them in order.

His task was not quite so easy as it looked, for the cows had a way of straying into the wood, and by the time he had brought one back another was off. He had gone some distance into the trees, after a black cow, which gave him more trouble than all the rest, when he heard the noise of horses' feet and, peeping through the leaves, he beheld the giant Rogéar seated on his mare, with the colt trotting behind. Round the giant's neck hung the golden bowl suspended from a chain, and in his hand he grasped the diamond lance, which gleamed like fire. But as soon as he was out of sight Peronnik sought in vain for traces of the path he had taken.

This happened not once but many times till Peronnik grew so used to him he never troubled to hide. But on each occasion he saw the giant the desire to possess the bowl and the lance became stronger.

ONE evening the boy was sitting alone on the edge of the forest, when a man with a white beard stopped beside him. 'Do you want to know the way to Kerglas?' asked the boy.

The man answered, 'I know it well.'

'You have been there without being killed by the magician?' cried Peronnik.

'Oh, he had nothing to fear from me,' replied the white-bearded man, 'I am Rogéar's elder brother, the wizard Bryak. When I wish to visit him I always pass this way, and as even I cannot go through the enchanted wood without losing myself, I call the colt to guide me.'

Stooping down, as he spoke, he traced three circles on the ground and murmured some words very low, which Peronnik could not hear. Then he added aloud:

'Colt, free to run and free to eat,
Colt, gallop fast until we meet,'

and instantly the colt appeared, frisking and jumping to the wizard, who threw a halter over his neck and leapt on his back.

PERONNIK kept silence at the farm about this adventure, but he understood very well that if he was ever to get to Kerglas he must first catch the colt which knew the way. Unhappily he had not heard the magic words uttered by the wizard, and he could not manage to draw the three circles, so if he was to summon the colt at all he must invent some other means of doing it.

All day long, while he was herding the cows, he thought and thought how he was to call the colt, for he felt sure that once on its back he could overcome the other dangers. Meantime he must be ready in case a chance should come, and he made his preparations at night, when everyone was asleep.

Remembering what he had seen the wizard do, he patched up an old halter that was hanging in a corner of the stable, twisted a rope of hemp to catch the colt's feet, and a net such as is used for snaring birds. Next he sewed roughly together some bits of cloth to serve as a pocket, and this he filled with glue and larks' feathers, a string of beads, a whistle of elder wood, and a slice of bread rubbed over with bacon fat. Then he went out to the path down which Rogéar, his mare and the colt always rode, and crumbled the bread on one side of it.

Punctual to their hour all three appeared, eagerly watched by Peronnik, who lay hidden in the bushes close by. Suppose it was useless; suppose the mare, and not the colt, ate the crumbs? Suppose—but no! the mare and her rider went safely by, vanishing round a corner, while the colt, trotting along with its head on the ground, smelt the bread and began greedily to lick up the pieces.

Oh, how good it was! Why had no one ever given it such food before, and so absorbed was the little beast, sniffing about after a few more crumbs, that it never heard Peronnik creep up till it felt the halter on its neck and the rope round its feet, and —in another moment—someone on its back.

Going as fast as the hobbles would allow, the colt turned into one of the wildest parts of the forest, while its rider sat trembling at the strange sights he saw. Sometimes the earth seemed to open in front of them and he was looking into a bottomless pit; sometimes the trees burst into flames and he found himself in the midst of a fire; often in the act of crossing a stream the water rose and threatened to sweep him away; and again, at the foot of a mountain, great rocks would roll toward him, as if they would crush him and his colt beneath their weight. To his dying day Peronnik never knew whether these things were real or if he only imagined them, but he pulled down his knitted cap to cover his eyes and trusted the colt to carry him down the right road.

At last the forest was left behind, and they came out on a wide plain where the air blew fresh and strong. The boy ventured to peep out, and found to his relief that the enchantments seemed to have ended, though a thrill of horror shot through him as he noticed the skeletons of men scattered over the plain, beside the skeletons of their horses. And what were those gray forms trotting away in the distance? Were they—could they be —wolves?

But vast though the plain seemed, it did not take long to cross, and very soon the colt entered a sort of park in which was standing a single apple tree, its branches bowed down to the ground with the weight of its fruit. In front was the korigan— the little fairy man—holding in his hand the fiery sword, which reduced to ashes everything it touched. At the sight of Peronnik, he uttered a piercing scream and raised his sword, but without appearing surprised the youth only lifted his cap, though he took care to remain at a little distance.

'Do not be alarmed,' said Peronnik, 'I am just on my way to Kerglas, as the noble Rogéar has begged me to come to him on business.'

'Begged you to come!' repeated the dwarf. 'And who, then, are you?'

'I am the new servant he has engaged, as you know very well,' answered Peronnik.

'I do not know at all,' rejoined the korigan sulkily, 'and you may be a robber for all I can tell.'

'I am so sorry,' replied Peronnik, 'but I may be wrong in calling myself a servant, for I am only a bird catcher. But do not delay me, I pray, for his highness the magician expects me, and as you see has lent me his colt so I may reach the castle all the quicker.'

At these words the korigan cast his eyes for the first time on the colt, which he knew to be the one belonging to the magician, and began to think that the young man was speaking the truth. After examining the steed, he studied the rider, who had such an innocent air that he appeared incapable of inventing a story. Still, the dwarf did not feel quite sure that all was right, and asked what the magician wanted with a bird catcher.

'From what he says, he wants one very badly,' replied Peronnik. 'He declares that all his grain and all the fruit in his garden at Kerglas are eaten up by the birds.'

'And how are you going to stop that, my fine fellow?' inquired the korigan.

Then Peronnik showed him the snare he had prepared, and remarked that no bird could possibly escape from it.

'That it just what I should like to be sure of,' answered the korigan. 'My apples are completely eaten up by blackbirds and thrushes. Lay your snare, and if you can manage to catch them, I will let you pass.'

'That is a fair bargain.' And as he spoke Peronnik jumped down and fastened his colt to a tree. Then, stooping, he fixed one end of the net to the trunk of the apple tree and called to the korigan to hold the other while he took out the pegs. The dwarf did as he was bid, when suddenly Peronnik threw the noose over his neck and drew it close, and the korigan was held as fast as any of the birds he wished to snare.

Shrieking with rage, he tried to undo the cord, but he only pulled the knot tighter. He had put down the sword on the grass, and Peronnik had been careful to fix the net on the other side of the tree, so it was now easy for him to pluck an apple and to mount his horse, without being hindered by the dwarf, whom he left to his fate.

WHEN they had left the plain behind them, Peronnik and his steed found themselves in a narrow valley in which was a grove of trees, full of all sorts of sweet-smelling things—roses of every color, yellow broom, pink honeysuckle—while above them all towered a wonderful scarlet pansy whose face bore a strange expression. This was the flower that laughs, and no one who looked at it could help laughing too. Peronnik's heart beat high at the thought that he had reached safely the second trial, and he gazed quite calmly at the lion with the mane of vipers twisting and twirling, who walked up and down in front of the grove.

The young man pulled up and removed his cap, for foolish though he was, he knew that when you have to do with people greater than yourself, a cap is more useful in the hand than on the head. Then, after wishing all kinds of good fortune to the lion and his family, he inquired if he was on the right road to Kerglas.

'And what is your business at Kerglas?' asked the lion with a growl and showing his teeth.

'With all respect,' answered Peronnik, pretending to be very frightened, 'I am the servant of a lady who is a friend of the noble Rogéar and sends him some larks for a pasty.'

'Larks?' cried the lion, licking his long whiskers. 'Why,

it must be a century since I have had any! Have you a large quantity with you?'

'As many as this bag will hold,' replied Peronnik, opening, as he spoke, the bag which he had filled with feathers and glue. And to prove what he said, he turned his back on the lion and began to imitate the song of a lark.

'Come,' exclaimed the lion, whose mouth watered, 'show me the birds! I should like to see if they are fat enough for my master.'

'I would do it with pleasure,' answered Peronnik, 'but if I once open the bag they will all fly away.'

'Well, open it wide enough for me to look in,' said the lion, drawing a little nearer.

Now this was just what Peronnik had been hoping for, so he held the bag while the lion opened it carefully and put his head right inside so he might get a good mouthful of larks. But the mass of feathers and glue stuck to him, and before he could pull his head out again Peronnik had drawn tight the cord and tied it in a knot that no man could untie.

Then, quickly gathering the flower that laughs, he rode off as fast as the colt could take him.

THE path soon led to the lake of the dragons, which he had to swim across. The colt, who was accustomed to it, plunged into the water without hesitation. But as soon as the dragons caught sight of Peronnik they approached from all parts of the lake in order to devour him.

This time Peronnik did not trouble to take off his cap, but he threw the beads he carried with him into the water, as you throw black corn to a duck, and with each bead that he swallowed a dragon turned on his back and died, so that the boy reached the other side without further trouble.

The valley guarded by the black man now lay before him, and from afar Peronik beheld him, chained by one foot to a rock at the entrance and holding the iron ball, which never missed its mark and always returned to its master's hand. In his head the man had six eyes that were never all shut at once, but kept watch one after the other. At this moment they were all open, and Peronnik knew well that if the black man caught a glimpse of him he would cast his ball.

So, hiding the colt behind a thicket of bushes, he crawled along a ditch and crouched close to the very rock to which the man was chained.

The day was hot, and after a while the man began to grow sleepy. Two of his eyes closed, and Peronnik sang gently. In a moment a third eye shut, and Peronnik sang on. The lid of a fourth eye dropped heavily, and then those of the fifth and the sixth. The black man was asleep altogether.

Then, on tiptoe, Peronnik crept back to the colt, which he led over soft moss past the sleeping man into the vale of pleasure, a delicious garden full of fruits that dangled before your mouth, fountains running with wine, and flowers chanting in soft little voices. Farther on, tables were spread with food, and girls dancing on the grass called to him to join them.

Peronnik heard and, scarcely knowing what he did, drew the colt to a slower pace. He sniffed greedily the smell of the dishes and raised his head the better to see the dancers. Another instant and he would have stopped altogether and been lost, like others before him, when suddenly there came to him like a vision the golden bowl and the diamond lance.

Drawing his whistle from his pocket, he blew it loudly to drown the sweet sounds about him, and ate what was left of his bread and bacon to still his craving for the magic fruits. His eyes he fixed steadily on the ears of the colt that he might not see the dancers.

In this way he was able to reach the end of the garden and at length perceived the castle of Kerglas, with the river between them which had only one ford. Would the lady be there, as the old man had told him? Yes, surely that was she, sitting on a rock, in a black satin dress, and her face the color of a Moorish woman's. The youth rode up, and took off his cap more politely than ever, and asked if she did not wish to cross the river.

'I was waiting for you to help me do so,' answered she. 'Come near, that I may get up behind you.'

Peronnik did as she bade him, and by the help of his arm, she jumped nimbly on to the back of the colt.

'Do you know how to kill the magician?' asked the lady, as they were crossing the ford.

'I thought that, being a magician, he was immortal, and that no one could kill him,' replied Peronnik.

'Persuade him to taste that apple, and he will die, and if that is not enough I will touch him with my finger, for I am the plague,' answered she.

'But if I kill him, how am I to get the golden bowl and the diamond lance that are hidden in the cellar without a key?' rejoined Peronnik.

'The flower that laughs opens all doors and lightens all darkness,' said the lady. And as she spoke, they reached the farther bank and advanced toward the castle.

In front of the entrance was a sort of tent supported on poles, and under it the giant was sitting, basking in the sun. As soon as he noticed the colt bearing Peronnik and the lady, he lifted his head, and cried in a voice of thunder:

'Why, it is surely the foolish one, riding my colt thirteen months old!'

'Greatest of magicians, you are right,' answered Peronnik.

'And how did you manage to catch him?' asked the giant.

'By repeating what I learned from your brother Bryak on the edge of the forest. I just said:

'Colt, free to run and free to eat,

Colt, gallop fast until we meet,'

and it came directly.'

'You know my brother, then?' inquired the giant. 'Tell me why he sent you here.'

'To bring you two gifts which he has just received from the country of the Moors,' answered Peronnik: 'the apple of delight and the woman of submission. If you eat the apple you will not desire anything else, and if you take the woman as your servant you will never wish for another.'

'Well, give me the apple, and bid the woman get down,' answered Rogéar.

The youth obeyed, but at the first taste of the apple the giant staggered, and as the long finger of the woman touched him he fell dead.

Leaving the magician where he lay, Peronnik entered the palace, bearing with him the flower that laughs. Fifty doors flew open before him, and at length he reached a long flight of steps which seemed to lead into the bowels of the earth. Down these he went till he came to a silver door without a bar or key. Then he held up high the flower that laughs, and the door slowly swung back, displaying a deep cavern which was as bright as day from the shining of the golden bowl and the diamond lance.

Peronnik hastily ran forward and hung the bowl round his neck from the chain which was attached to it and took the lance in his hand. As he did so, the ground shook beneath him, and with an awful rumbling the palace disappeared, and Peronnik found himself standing close to the forest where he led the cattle to graze.

THOUGH darkness was coming on, Peronnik never thought of entering the farm, but followed the road which led to the court of the Duke of Brittany. As he passed through the town of Vannes he stopped at a tailor's shop and bought a beautiful costume of brown velvet and a white horse, which he paid for with a handful of gold that he had picked up in the corridor of the castle of Kerglas. Thus he made his way to the city of Nantes, which at that moment was besieged by the French.

A little way off, Peronnik stopped and looked about him. For miles round the country was bare, for the enemy had cut down every tree and burnt every blade of corn. Foolish though he might be, Peronnik was able to grasp that inside the gates men were dying of famine. He was still gazing with horror, when a trumpeter appeared on the walls and, after blowing a loud blast, announced that the duke would adopt as his heir the man who could drive the French out of the country.

On the four sides of the city the trumpeter blew his blast. And the last time Peronnik, who had ridden up as close as he might, answered him.

'You need blow no more,' said he, 'for I myself will free the town from her enemies.'

Turning to a soldier who came running up, waving his sword, he touched him with the magic lance, and he fell dead on the spot. The men who were following stood still, amazed. Their comrade's armor had not been pierced, of that they were sure, yet he was dead, as if he had been struck to the heart. But before they had time to recover from their astonishment, Peronnik cried out:

'You see how my foes will fare; now behold what I can do

for my friends.' Stooping down, he laid the golden bowl against the mouth of the soldier, who sat up as well as ever. Then, jumping his horse across the trench, he entered the gate of the city, which had opened wide enough to receive him.

The news of these marvels quickly spread through the town and put fresh spirit into the garrison, so that they declared themselves able to fight under the command of the young stranger. And as the bowl restored all the dead Bretons to life, Peronnik soon had an army large enough to drive away the French and fulfilled his promise of delivering his country.

As for the bowl and the lance, no one knows what became of them, but some say that Bryak the sorcerer managed to steal them again, and that anyone who wishes to possess them must seek them as Peronnik did.

[From *Le Foyer Breton,* by Emile Souvestre.]

The White Doe

ONCE UPON A TIME
there lived a king and queen who loved each other dearly, and
would have been perfectly happy if they had only had a little
son or daughter to play with. They never talked about it, and
always pretended there was nothing in the world to wish for;
but, sometimes, when they looked at other people's children,
their faces grew sad, and their courtiers and attendants knew
the reason why.

One day the queen was sitting alone by the side of a waterfall which sprang from some rocks in the large park adjoining
the castle. She was feeling more than usually miserable and
had sent away her ladies that no one might witness her grief.
Suddenly she heard a rustling movement in the pool below the
waterfall and, on glancing up, she saw a large crab climbing
on to a stone beside her.

'Great queen,' said the crab, 'I am here to tell you that the
desire of your heart will soon be granted. But first you must
permit me to lead you to the palace of the fairies which, though
hard by, has never been seen by mortal eyes because of the
thick clouds that surround it. When there you will know more;
that is, if you will trust yourself to me.'

The queen had never before heard a crab speak and was dumb with surprise. However, she was so enchanted at its words that she smiled sweetly and held out her hand. It was taken, not by the crab, which had stood there only a moment before, but by a little old woman smartly dressed in white and crimson, with green ribbons in her gray hair. And, wonderful to say, not a drop of water fell from her clothes.

The old woman ran lightly down a path along which the queen had been a hundred times before, but it seemed so different she could hardly believe it was the same. Instead of having to push her way through nettles and brambles, roses and jasmine hung about her head, while under her feet the ground was sweet with violets. The orange trees were so tall and thick that, even at midday, the sun was never too hot, and at the end of the path was a glimmer of something so dazzling the queen had to shade her eyes and peep at it only between her fingers.

'What can it be?' she asked, turning to her guide.

'Oh, that is the fairies' palace, and here are some of them coming to meet us.'

As the little old woman spoke the gates swung back and six fairies approached, each bearing in her hand a flower made of precious stones, but so like a real one that it was only by touching could you tell the difference.

'Madam,' they said, 'we know not how to thank you for this mark of your confidence but have the happiness to tell you that in a short time you will have a little daughter.'

The queen was so enchanted at this news that she nearly fainted wtih joy. But when she was able to speak, she poured out all her gratitude to the fairies for their promised gift.

'And now,' she said, 'I ought not to stay any longer, for my husband will think that I have run away or that some evil beast has devoured me.'

I<small>N</small> a little while it happened just as the fairies had foretold, and a baby girl was born in the palace. Of course both the king and queen were delighted, and the child was called Désirée, which means 'desired,' for she had been desired for five long years before her birth.

At first the queen could think of nothing but her little daughter, but then she remembered the fairies who had sent it to her. Bidding her ladies bring her the posy of jeweled flowers, which had been given her at the fairies' palace, she took each flower in her hand and called it by name and, in turn, each fairy appeared before her.

But, as unluckily often happens, the one to whom she owed most, the crab-fairy, was forgotten, and by this, as in the case of other babies you have read about, much mischief was wrought.

However, for the moment all was gaiety in the palace, and everybody inside ran to the windows to watch the fairies' carriages, for no two were alike. One had a car of ebony, drawn by white pigeons, another was lying back in her ivory chariot, driving ten black crows, while the rest had chosen rare woods or many-colored sea shells, with scarlet and blue macaws, long-tailed peacocks, or green lovebirds for horses. These carriages were only used on occasions of state, for when they went to war flying dragons, fiery serpents, lions or leopards, took the place of the beautiful birds.

The fairies entered the queen's chamber followed by little dwarfs who carried their presents and looked much prouder than their mistresses. One by one their burdens were spread upon the ground, and no one had ever seen such lovely things. Everything a baby could possibly wear or play with was there and, besides, they had other and more precious gifts to give her, which only children who have fairies for godmothers can ever hope to possess.

They were all gathered round the heap of pink cushions on which the baby lay asleep, when a shadow seemed to fall between them and the sun, while a cold wind blew through the room. Everybody looked up, and there was the crab-fairy, who had grown as tall as the ceiling in her anger.

'So I am forgotten!' cried she, in a voice so loud that the queen trembled as she heard it. 'Who was it soothed you in your trouble? Who was it led you to the fairies? Who was it brought you back in safety to your home again? Yet I am overlooked, while these, who have done nothing in comparison, are petted and thanked.'

The queen, almost dumb with terror, in vain tried to think of some explanation or apology. But there was none, and she could only confess her fault and implore forgiveness. The fairies also did their best to soften the wrath of their sister and knowing that, like many plain people who are not fairies, she was very vain, they entreated her to drop her crab's disguise and to become once more the charming person they were accustomed to see.

For some time the enraged fairy would listen to nothing; but at length the flatteries began to take effect. The crab's shell fell from her, she shrank into her usual size and lost some of her fierce expression.

'Well,' she said, 'I will not cause the princess' death, as I had meant to do, but at the same time she will have to bear the punishment of her mother's fault, as many other children have done before her. The sentence I pass upon her is that if she is allowed to see one ray of daylight before her fifteenth birthday she will rue it bitterly, and it may perhaps cost her her life.'

With these words she vanished by the window through which she came, while the fairies comforted the weeping queen, and took counsel how best the princess might be kept safe during her childhood.

At the end of half an hour they had made up their minds what to do, and at the command of the fairies, a beautiful palace sprang up, close to that of the king and queen, but different from every other palace in the world, in having no windows, and only a door right under the earth. However, once within, daylight was hardly missed, so brilliant were the multitudes of tapers that were burning on the walls.

Now up to this time the princess' history has been like the history of many a princess you have read about; but, when the period of her imprisonment was nearly over, her fortunes took another turn. For almost fifteen years the fairies had taken care of her, amused her and taught her, so that when she came into the daylight world she might be no whit behind the daughters of other kings in all that makes a princess charming and accomplished.

They all loved her dearly, but the fairy Tulip loved her most of all; and as the princess' fifteenth birthday drew near, the fairy began to tremble lest something terrible should happen—some accident which had not been foreseen.

'Do not let her out of your sight,' said Tulip to the queen, 'and meanwhile, let her portrait be painted and carried to the neighboring courts, as is the custom, in order that the kings may see how far her beauty exceeds that of every other princess and that they may demand her in marriage for their sons.'

And so it was done and, as the fairy had prophesied, all the young princes fell in love with the picture. But the last one to whom it was shown could think of nothing else and refused to let it be removed from his chamber, where he spent whole days gazing at it.

The king, his father, was much surprised at the change

which had come over his son, who generally passed all his time in hunting or hawking, and his anxiety was increased by a conversation he overheard between two of his courtiers that they feared the prince must be going out of his mind, so moody had he become. Without losing a moment the king went to visit his son, and no sooner had he entered the room than the young man flung himself at his father's feet.

'You have betrothed me already to a bride I can never love!' cried he. 'But if you will not consent to break off the match and ask for the hand of the Princess Désirée, I shall die of misery, thankful to be alive no longer.'

These words much displeased the king, who felt that, in breaking off the marriage already arranged, he would almost certainly be bringing on his subjects a long and bloody war. So without answering, he turned away, hoping that a few days might bring his son to reason. But the prince's condition grew rapidly so much worse that the king, in despair, promised to send an embassy at once to Désirée's father.

This news cured the young man in an instant of all his ills, and he began to plan out every detail of dress and of horses and carriages which were necessary to make the train of the envoy, whose name was Becasigue, as splendid as possible. He longed to form part of the embassy himself, if only in the disguise of a page; but this the king would not allow, and so the prince had to content himself with searching the kingdom for everything that was rare and beautiful to send to the princess. Indeed, he arrived, just as the embassy was starting, with his portrait, which had been painted in secret by the court painter.

The king and queen wished for nothing better than that their daughter should marry into such a great and powerful family and received the ambassador with every sign of welcome. They even wished him to see the Princess Désirée, but this was prevented by the fairy Tulip, who feared some ill might come of it.

'And be sure you tell him,' added she, 'that the marriage cannot be celebrated till she is fifteen years old, or else some terrible misfortune will happen to the child.'

So when Becasigue, surrounded by his train, made a formal request that the Princess Désirée might be given in marriage to his master's son, the king replied that he was much honored and would gladly give his consent, but that no one could even see the princess till her fifteenth birthday, as the spell laid upon her in her cradle by a spiteful fairy would not cease to work till that was past.

The ambassador was greatly surprised and disappointed, but he knew too much about fairies to venture to disobey them, therefore he had to content himself with presenting the prince's portrait to the queen, who lost no time in carrying it to the princess. As the girl took it in her hands it suddenly spoke, as it had been taught to do, and uttered a compliment of the most delicate and charming sort, which made the princess flush with pleasure.

'How would you like to have a husband like that?' asked the queen, laughing.

'As if I knew anything about husbands!' replied Désirée, who had long ago guessed the business of the ambassador.

'Well, he will be your husband in three months,' answered the queen, ordering the prince's presents to be brought in.

The princess was very pleased with them and admired them greatly, but the queen noticed that all the while her eyes constantly strayed from the softest silks and most brilliant jewels to the portrait of the prince.

The ambassador, finding there was no hope of his being allowed to see the princess, took his leave and returned to his own court; but here a new difficulty appeared. The prince, though transported with joy at the thought that Désirée was indeed to be his bride, was bitterly disappointed that she had not been allowed to return with Becasigue, as he had foolishly expected; and never having been taught to deny himself anything or to control his feelings, he fell as ill as he had done before. He would eat nothing nor take pleasure in anything, but lay all day on a heap of cushions, gazing at the picture of the princess.

'If I have to wait three months before I can marry the princess I shall die!' was all this spoilt boy would say.

At length the king, in despair, resolved to send a fresh embassy to Désirée's father to implore him to permit the marriage to be celebrated at once. 'I would have presented my prayer in person,' he added in his letter, 'but my great age and infirmities do not suffer me to travel; however my envoy has orders to agree to any arrangement that you may propose.'

On his arrival at the palace Becasigue pleaded his young master's cause as fervently as his kingly father could have done and entreated that the princess might be consulted in the matter. The queen hastened to the marble tower, and told her daughter of the sad state of the prince. Désirée sank down fainting at the news, but soon came to herself again and set about inventing a plan which would enable her to go to the prince without risking the doom pronounced over her by the wicked fairy.

'I see!' she exclaimed joyfully at last. 'Let a carriage be built through which no light can come, and let it be brought into my room. I will then get into it and we can travel swiftly during the night and arrive before dawn at the palace of the prince. Once there, I can remain in some underground chamber, where no light can come.'

'Ah, how clever you are,' cried the queen, clasping her in her arms. And she hurried away to tell the king.

'What a wife our prince will have!' said Becasigue bowing low. 'I must hasten back with the tidings and to prepare the underground chamber for the princess.' And so he took his leave.

In a few days the carriage commanded by the princess was ready. It was of green velvet, scattered over with large golden thistles, and lined inside with silver brocade embroidered with pink roses. It had no windows, of course, but the fairy Tulip, whose counsel had been asked, had managed to light it up with a soft glow that came no one knew whither.

It was carried straight up into the great hall of the tower, and the princess stepped into it, followed by her faithful maid of honor, Eglantine, and by her lady-in-waiting Cérisette, who also had fallen in love with the prince's portrait and was bitterly jealous of her mistress. The fourth place in the carriage was filled by Cérisette's mother, who had been sent by the queen to look after the three young people.

Now the Fairy of the Fountain was the godmother of the Princess Nera, to whom the prince had been betrothed before the picture of Désirée had made him faithless. She was very angry at the slight put upon her godchild and from that moment kept careful watch on the Princess Désirée. In this journey she saw her chance, and it was she who, invisible, sat beside them and put bad thoughts into the minds of both Cérisette and her mother.

The way to the city where the prince lived ran for the most part through a thick forest, and every night when there was no moon, and not a single star could be seen through the trees, the guards who traveled with the princess opened the carriage to give it an airing. This went on for several days, till only twelve hours' journey lay between them and the palace.

Then Cérisette persuaded her mother to cut a great hole in the side of the carriage with a sharp knife which she herself had brought along. In the forest the darkness was so intense that no one perceived what she had done, but when they left the last trees behind them and emerged into the open country, the sun was up, and for the first time since her babyhood, Désirée found herself in the light of day.

She looked up in surprise at the dazzling brilliance that streamed through the hole, then gave a sigh which seemed to come from her heart. The carriage door swung back, as if by magic, and a white doe sprang out and in a moment was lost to sight in the forest. But, quick as she was, Eglantine, her maid of honor, had time to see where she went and jumped from the carriage in pursuit of her, followed at a distance by the guards.

Cérisette and her mother looked at each other in surprise and joy. They could hardly believe in their good fortune, for everything had happened exactly as they wished. The first thing to be done was to conceal the hole which had been cut, and when this was managed—with the help of the angry Fairy of the Fountain, though they did not know it—Cérisette hastened to take off her own clothes and put on those of the princess, placing the crown of diamonds on her head. She found this heavier than she expected; but then, she had never been accustomed to wear crowns, which makes all the difference.

At the gates of the city the carriage was stopped by a guard of honor sent by the king as an escort to his son's bride. Though Cérisette and her mother could of course see nothing of what was going on outside, they heard plainly the shouts of welcome from the crowds along the streets.

The carriage stopped at length in the vast hall which Beca-sigue had prepared for the reception of the princess. The grand chamberlain and the lord high steward were awaiting her, and when the false bride stepped into the brilliantly lighted room, they bowed low and said they had orders to inform his highness the moment she arrived. The prince, whom the strict etiquette of the court had prevented from being present in the underground hall, was burning with impatience in his own apartments.

'So she has come!' cried he, throwing down the bow he had been pretending to mend. 'Well, was I not right? Is she not a miracle of beauty and grace? And has she her equal in the whole world?'

The ministers looked at each other and made no reply. At length the chamberlain, who was the bolder of the two, observed:

'My lord, as to her beauty, you can judge of that for yourself. No doubt it is as great as you say, but at present it seems to have suffered, as is natural, from the fatigues of the journey.'

This was certainly not what the prince expected to hear. Could the portrait have flattered her? He had known of such things before, and a cold shiver ran through him. But with an effort he kept silent from further questioning, and only said:

'Has the king been told the princess is in the palace?'

'Yes, Your Highness. He has probably already joined her.'

'Then I will go too,' said the prince.

Weak as he was from his long illness, the prince descended the staircase, supported by the ministers, and entered the room just in time to hear his father's loud cry of astonishment and disgust at the sight of Cérisette.

'There has been treachery at work,' he exclaimed, while the prince leaned, dumb with horror, against the doorpost. But the lady's mother, who had been prepared for something of the sort, advanced, holding in her hand the letters which the king and queen had entrusted to her.

'This is the Princess Désirée,' said she, pretending to have heard nothing, 'and I have the honor to present to you these letters from my liege lord and lady, together with the casket containing the princess' jewels.'

The king did not move or answer her, so the prince, leaning on the arm of Becasigue, approached a little closer to the false princess, hoping against hope that his eyes had deceived him. But the longer he looked the more he agreed with his father that there was treason somewhere, for in no single respect did the portrait resemble the woman before him. Cérisette was so tall that the dress of the princess did not reach her ankles, and so thin that her bones showed through the stuff. Besides that her nose was too large, and her teeth black and ugly.

In his turn, the prince stood rooted to the spot. At last he spoke, and his words were addressed to his father and not to the bride who had come so far to marry him.

'We have been deceived,' he said, 'and it will cost me my life.' And he leaned so heavily on the envoy that Becasigue feared he was going to faint and hastily laid him on the floor. For some minutes no one could attend to anybody but the prince. But as soon as he revived, the mother made herself heard.

'Oh, my lovely princess, why did we ever leave home?' cried she. 'But the king your father will avenge the insults that have been heaped on you when we tell him how you have been treated.'

'I will tell him myself,' replied the king in wrath. 'He promised me a wonder of beauty, he has sent me a skeleton. I am not surprised that he has kept her for fifteen years hidden from the eyes of the world. Take them both away,' he continued, turning to his guards, 'and lodge them in the state prison. There is something more I have to learn of this matter.'

His orders were obeyed, and the prince, loudly bewailing his sad fate, was led back to his bed, where for many days he lay in a high fever. At length he slowly began to gain strength, but his sorrow was still so great that he could not bear the sight of a strange face, and shuddered at the notion of taking his proper part in the court ceremonies.

Unknown to the king, or to anybody but Becasigue, he planned that, as soon as he was able, he would make his escape and pass the rest of his life in some solitary place. It was some weeks before he had regained his health sufficiently to carry out his design. But finally, one beautiful starlight night, the two friends stole away, and when the king woke next morning he found a letter lying by his bed, saying that his son had gone, he knew not whither.

He wept bitter tears at the news, for he loved the prince dearly. But he felt that perhaps the young man had done wisely, and he trusted to time and Becasigue's influence to bring the wanderer home.

And while these things were happening, what had become of the white doe? Though when she sprang from the carriage she was aware that some unkind fate has changed her into an animal, yet, till she saw herself in a stream, she had no idea what it was.

'Is it really, I, Désirée?' she said to herself, weeping. 'What wicked fairy can have treated me so? Shall I never, never take my own shape again? My only comfort is that, in this great forest full of lions and serpents, my life will be a short one.'

Now the fairy Tulip was as much grieved at the sad fate of the princess as Désirée's own mother could have been if she had known of it. Still, she could not help feeling that if the king and queen had listened to her advice the girl would by this time be safely in the walls of her new home. However, she loved Désirée too much to let her suffer more than could be helped, and it was she who guided Eglantine to the place where the white doe was standing, cropping the grass which was her dinner.

At the sound of footsteps the pretty creature lifted her head, and when she saw her faithful companion approaching she bounded toward her and rubbed her head on Eglantine's shoulder. The maid of honor was surprised; but she was fond of animals and stroked the white doe tenderly, speaking gently to her all the while.

Suddenly the beautiful creature lifted her head and looked up into Eglantine's face, with tears streaming from her eyes. A thought flashed through her mind, and quick as lightning the girl flung herself on her knees, and lifting the animal's feet kissed them one by one.

'My Princess! O my dear Princess!' cried she. Again the white doe rubbed her head against her, for though the spiteful fairy had taken away her power of speech, she had not deprived her of her reason!

All day long the two remained together, and when Eglantine grew hungry she was led by the white doe to a part of the forest where pears and peaches grew in abundance. But, as night came on, the maid of honor was filled with the terror of wild beasts which had beset the princess during her first night in the forest.

'Is there no hut or cave we could go into?' asked Eglantine. But the doe only shook her head and the two sat down and wept with fright.

The fairy Tulip who, in spite of her anger, was very soft-hearted, was touched at their distress, and flew quickly to their help.

'I cannot take away the spell altogether,' she said, 'for the Fairy of the Fountain is stronger than I. But I can shorten the time of your punishment and am able to make it less hard, for as soon as darkness falls you shall resume your own shape.'

To think that by-and-by she would cease to be a white doe—indeed, that she would at once cease to be one during the night—was for the present joy enough for Désirée, and she skipped about on the grass in the prettiest manner.

'Go straight down the path in front of you,' continued the fairy, smiling as she watched her, 'go straight down the path and you will soon reach a little hut where you will find shelter.'

And with these words she vanished, leaving her hearers happier than they ever thought they could be again.

An old woman was standing at the door of the hut when Eglantine drew near, with the white doe trotting by her side.

'Good evening!' she said. 'Could you give me a night's lodging for myself and my doe?'

'Certainly I can,' replied the old woman. And she led them into a room with two little white beds, so clean and comfortable that it made them sleepy even to look at them.

The door had hardly closed behind the old woman when the sun sank below the horizon, and Désirée became a girl again.

'Oh, Eglantine! What should I have done if you had not followed me?' she cried. And she flung herself into her friend's arms in a transport of delight.

Early in the morning Eglantine was awakened by the sound of someone scratching at the door, and on opening her eyes she saw the white doe struggling to get out. The little creature looked up into her face and nodded her head as the maid of honor unfastened the latch, but bounded away into the woods, and was lost to sight in a moment.

MEANWHILE, the prince and Becasigue were wandering through the wood, till at last the prince grew so tired that he lay down under a tree and told Becasigue he had better go in search of food and of some place where they could sleep. Becasigue had not gone very far, when a turn of the path brought him face to face with the old woman, who was feeding her doves before her cottage.

'Could you give me some milk and fruit?' asked he. 'I am very hungry myself and, besides, I have left a friend behind me who is still weak from illness.'

'Certainly I can,' answered the old woman. 'But come and sit down in my kitchen while I catch the goat and milk it.'

Becasigue was glad enough to do as he was bidden, and in a few minutes the old woman returned with a basket brimming over with oranges and grapes.

'If your friend has been ill he should not pass the night in the forest,' said she. 'I have a room in my hut—tiny enough, it is true; but better than nothing, and to that you are both heartily welcome.'

Becasigue thanked her warmly. By this time it was almost sunset, and he set out to fetch the prince. It was while he was absent that Eglantine and the white doe entered the hut, and having, of course, no idea that in the very next room was the man whose childish impatience had been the cause of all their troubles.

In spite of his fatigue, the prince slept badly, and directly it was light he rose. Bidding Becasigue remain where he was, as he wished to be alone, he strolled out into the forest. He walked on slowly, just as his fancy led him till, suddenly, he came to a wide open space, and in the middle was the white doe quietly eating her breakfast.

She bounded off at the sight of a man, but not before the prince, who had fastened on his bow without thinking, had let fly several arrows, which the fairy Tulip took care should do her no harm. But, quickly as she ran, Désirée soon felt her strength failing her, for fifteen years of life in a tower had not taught her how to exercise her limbs.

Luckily, the prince was too weak to follow her far, and a turn of a path brought her close to the hut, where Eglantine was awaiting her. Panting for breath, she entered their room, and flung herself down on the floor.

When it was dark again, and she was once more the Princess Désirée, she told Eglantine what had befallen her.

'I feared the Fairy of the Fountain and the cruel beasts,' said she, 'but somehow I never thought of the dangers that I ran from men. I do not know now what saved me.'

'You must stay quietly here till the time of your punishment is over,' answered Eglantine. But when the morning dawned, and the girl turned into a doe, the longing for the forest came over her and she sprang away as before.

As soon as the prince was awake he hastened to the place where, only the day before, he had found the white doe feeding; but of course she had taken care to go in the opposite direction. Much disappointed, he tried first one green path and then another, and at last, wearied with walking, he threw himself down and fell fast asleep.

Just at this moment the white doe sprang out of a thicket near by and started back trembling when she beheld her enemy lying there. Yet, instead of turning to fly, something bade her go and look at him unseen. As she gazed a thrill ran through her, for she felt that, worn and wasted though he was by illness, it was the face of her destined husband. Gently stooping over him she kissed his forhead, and at her touch he awoke.

For a minute they looked at each other, and to his amazement the prince recognized the white doe which had escaped him the previous day. But in an instant the animal was aroused to a sense of her danger, and she fled with all her strength into the thickest part of the forest. Quick as lightning the prince was on her track, but this time it was with no wish to kill or even wound the beautiful creature.

'Pretty doe! Pretty doe! Stop! I won't hurt you,' cried he, but his words were carried away by the wind.

At length the doe could run no more, and when the prince reached her, she was lying stretched out on the grass, waiting for her death blow. But instead the prince knelt at her side, stroked her, and bade her fear nothing, as he would take care of her. So he fetched a little water from the stream in his horn hunting cup, then, cutting some branches from the trees, he twisted them into a litter, which he covered with moss, and laid the white doe gently on it.

For a long time they remained thus, but when Désirée saw by the way that the light struck the trees, that the sun must be near its setting, she was filled with alarm lest the darkness should fall, and the prince should behold her in her human shape.

'No, he must not see me for the first time here,' she said to herself, and instantly began to plan how to get rid of him. Then she opened her mouth and let her tongue hang out, as if she were dying of thirst, and the prince, as she expected, hastened to the stream to get her some more water.

When he returned, the white doe was gone.

That night Désirée confessed to Eglantine that her pursuer

was no other than the prince, and that far from flattering him, the portrait had never done him justice.

'Is it not hard to meet him in this shape,' she wept, 'when we both love each other so much?'

But Eglantine comforted her, and reminded her that in a short time all would be well.

The prince was very angry at the flight of the white doe, for whom he had taken so much trouble, and returning to the cottage he poured out his adventures and his wrath to Becasigue, who could not help smiling.

'She shall not escape me again!' cried the prince. 'If I hunt her every day for a year, I will have her at last.' And in this frame of mind he went to bed.

When the white doe entered the forest next morning, she had not made up her mind whether she would go and meet the prince, or whether she would shun him and hide in the thickets of which he knew nothing. She decided that the last plan was the best; and so it would have been if the prince had not taken the very same direction in search of her.

Quite by accident he caught sight of her white skin shining through the bushes, and at the same instant she heard a twig snap under his feet. In a moment she was up and away, but the prince, not knowing how else to capture her, aimed an arrow at her leg, which brought her to the ground.

The young man felt like a murderer as he ran hastily up to where the white doe lay and did his best to soothe the pain she felt, which, in reality, was the last part of the punishment sent by the Fairy of the Fountain. First he brought her some water, and then he fetched some healing herbs, and having crushed them in his hands, laid them on the wound.

'Ah, what a wretch I was to have hurt you!' cried he, resting her head upon his knees. 'And now you will hate me and fly from me forever!'

For some time the doe lay quietly where she was, but, as before, she remembered that the hour of her transformation was near. She struggled to her feet, but the prince would not think of her walking, and hoping the old woman might be able to dress her wound better than he could, he took the white doe in his arms to carry her back to the hut. But, small as she was, she made herself so heavy that, after staggering a few steps under her weight, he laid her down and tied her fast to a tree with some of the ribbons off his hat. This done he went away to get help.

Meanwhile, Eglantine had grown very uneasy at the long absence of her mistress and had come out to look for her. Just as the prince passed out of sight the fluttering ribbons danced before her eyes, and she descried her beautiful princess bound to a tree. With all her might she worked at the knots, but not a single one could she undo, though all appeared so easy. She was still busy with them when a voice behind her said:

'Pardon me, fair lady, but it is my doe you are trying to steal!'

'Excuse me, good knight' answered Eglantine hardly glancing at him, 'but it is my doe that is tied up here! And if you wish for a proof of it, you can see if she knows me or not. Touch my heart, my little one,' she continued, dropping on her knees. And the doe lifted up its forefoot and laid it on her side. 'Now put your arms round my neck, and sigh.' And again the doe did as she was bid.

'You are right,' said the prince, 'but it is with sorrow I give her up to you, for though I have wounded her yet I love her deeply.'

To this Eglantine answered nothing, but carefully raising up the doe, she led her slowly to the hut.

Now both the prince and Becasigue were quite unaware that the old woman had any guests beside themselves and, following afar, were much surprised to behold Eglantine and her charge enter the cottage. They lost no time in questioning the old woman, who replied that she knew nothing about the lady and her white doe, who slept next the chamber occupied by the prince and his friend, but that they were very quiet and paid her well. Then she went back to her kitchen.

'Do you know,' said Becasigue, when they were alone, 'I am certain that the lady we saw is the maid of honor to the Princess Désirée, whom I met at the palace. And, as her room is next to this, it will be easy to make a small hole through which I can satisfy myself whether I am right or not.'

So, taking a knife out of his pocket, he began to saw away the woodwork. The girls heard the grating noise, but fancying it was a mouse, paid no attention, and Becasigue was left in peace to pursue his work. At length the hole was large enough for him to peep through, and the sight was one to strike him dumb with amazement. He had guessed truly: the tall lady was Eglantine herself; but the other—where had he seen her? Ah! Now he knew—it was the lady of the portrait!

Désirée, in a flowing dress of green silk, was lying stretched out upon cushions, and as Eglantine bent over her to bathe the wounded leg, she began to talk:

'Oh! let me die,' cried she, 'rather than go on leading this life! You cannot tell the misery of being a beast all the day, and unable to speak to the man I love, to whose impatience I owe my cruel fate. Yet, even so, I cannot bring myself to hate him.'

These words, low though they were spoken, reached Becasigue, who could hardly believe his ears. He stood silent for a moment; then, crossing to the window out of which the prince was gazing, he took his arm and led him across the room. A single glance was sufficient to show the prince that it was indeed Désirée; and how another had come to the palace bearing her name, at that instant he neither knew nor cared. Stealing on tiptoe from the room he knocked at the next door, which was opened by Eglantine, who thought it was the old woman bearing their supper.

She started back at the sight of the prince, whom this time she also recognized. But he thrust her aside and flung himself at the feet of Désirée, to whom he poured out all his heart!

Dawn found them still conversing; and the sun was high in the heavens before the princess perceived that she had retained her human form. Ah! how happy she was when she knew that the days of her punishment were over, and with a glad voice she told the prince the tale of her enchantment.

So the story ended well after all; and the fairy Tulip, who turned out to be the old woman of the hut, made the young couple such a wedding feast as had never been seen since the world began. And everybody was delighted, except Cérisette and her mother, who were put in a boat and carried to a small island, where they had to work hard for their living.

[From *Les Contes des Fées*, by Madame d'Aulnoy.]

The Frog and the Lion Fairy

ONCE UPON A TIME there lived a king who was always at war with his neighbors, which was very strange, as he was a good and kind man, quite content with his own country and not wanting to seize land belonging to other people. Perhaps he may have tried too much to please everybody, and that often ends in pleasing nobody; but, at any rate, he found himself, at the end of a hard struggle, defeated in battle and obliged to fall back behind the walls of his capital city. Once there, he began to make preparations for a long siege, and the first thing he did was to plan how best to send his wife to a place of security.

The queen, who loved her husband dearly, would gladly have remained with him and shared his dangers, but he would not allow it. So they parted, with many tears, and the queen set out with a strong guard to a fortified castle on the outskirts of a great forest, some two hundred miles distant. She cried nearly all the way, and when she arrived she cried still more, for everything in the castle was dusty and old, and outside there was only a graveled courtyard, and the king had forbidden her to go beyond the walls without at least two soldiers to take care of her.

Now the queen had only been married a few months, and in her own home she had been used to walk and ride all over the hills without any attendants at all; so she felt very dull being shut up in this way. However, she bore it for a long while because it was the king's wish, but when time passed and there were no signs of the war drifting in the direction of the castle, she grew bolder and sometimes strayed outside the walls, in the direction of the forest.

Then came a dreadful period, when news from the king ceased entirely.

'He must surely be ill or dead,' thought the poor queen, who even now was only sixteen. 'I can bear it no longer, and if I do not get a letter from him soon, I shall leave this horrible place, and go back to see what is the matter. Oh! I do wish I had never come away!'

So, without telling anyone what she intended to do, she ordered a little low carriage to be built, something like a sledge, only it was on two wheels—just big enough to hold one person.

'I am tired of being always in the castle,' she said to her attendants, 'and I mean to hunt a little. Quite close by, of course,' she added, seeing the anxious look on their faces. 'And there is no reason that you should not hunt too.'

All the faces brightened at that, for, to tell the truth, they found the days nearly as dull as their mistress did. So the queen had her way, and two beautiful horses were brought from the stable to draw the little chariot. At first the queen took care to keep near the rest of the hunt, but gradually she stayed away longer and longer, and at last, one morning, she took advantage of the appearance of a wild boar, after which her whole court instantly galloped, to turn into a path in the opposite direction.

Unluckily, it did not happen to lead toward the king's palace, where she intended to go, but she was so afraid her flight would be noticed that she whipped up her horses till they ran away.

When she understood what was happening, the poor young queen was terribly frightened and, dropping the reins, clung to the side of the chariot. The horses, thus left without any control, dashed blindly against a tree, and the queen was flung out on the ground, where she lay for some minutes unconscious.

At length, a rustling sound near her caused her to open her eyes. Before her stood a huge woman, almost a giantess, clothed only in a lion's skin, which was thrown over her shoulders, while a dried snake's skin was plaited into her hair. In one hand she held a club on which she leaned, and in the other a quiver full of arrows.

At the sight of this strange figure the queen thought she must be dead and gazing on an inhabitant of another world. So she murmured softly to herself:

'I am not surprised that people are so loth to die when they know that they will see such horrible creatures.' But, low as she spoke, the giantess caught the words, and began to laugh.

'Oh, don't be afraid; you are still alive, and perhaps, after all, you may be sorry for it. I am the Lion Fairy, and you are going to spend the rest of your days with me in my palace, which is quite near this. So come along.' But the queen shrank back in horror.

'Oh, Madam Lion, take me back, I pray you, to my castle. Fix what ransom you like, for my husband will pay it, whatever it is.'

But the giantess shook her head.

'I am rich enough already,' she answered, 'but I am often dull, and I think you may amuse me a little.' And, so saying, she changed her shape into that of a lion, and throwing the

queen across her back, she went down the ten thousand steps that led to her palace.

The lion had reached the center of the earth before she stopped in front of a house, lighted with lamps, and built on the edge of a lake of quicksilver. In this lake various huge monsters might be seen playing or fighting—the queen did not know which—and around flew rooks and ravens, uttering dismal croaks. In the distance was a mountain down whose sides waters slowly coursed—these were the tears of unhappy lovers —and nearer the gate were trees without either fruit or flowers, while nettles and brambles covered the ground. If the castle had been gloomy, what did the queen feel about this?

For some days the queen was so much shaken by all she had gone through that she lay with her eyes closed, unable either to move or speak. When she was better, the Lion Fairy told her that if she liked she could build herself a cabin, as she would have to spend her life in that place. At these words the queen burst into tears and implored her gaoler to put her to death rather than condemn her to such a life. But the Lion Fairy only laughed and counseled her to try and make herself pleasant, as many worse things might befall her.

'Is there no way in which I can touch your heart?' asked the poor queen in despair.

'Well, if you really wish to please me you will make me a pasty out of the stings of bees, and be sure it is good.'

'But I don't see any bees,' answered the queen, looking round.

'Oh, no, there aren't any,' replied her tormentor; 'but you will have to find them all the same.' And, so saying, she went away.

'After all, what does it matter?' said the queen to herself. 'I have only one life and I can but lose it.' And not caring what she did, she left the palace and, seating herself under a yew tree, poured out all her grief.

'Oh, my dear husband,' she wept, 'what will you think when you come to the castle to fetch me and find me gone? Rather a thousand times you should fancy me dead than imagine I had forgotten you! Ah, how fortunate that the broken chariot should be lying in the wood, for then you may grieve for me as one devoured by wild beasts. And if another should take my place in your heart—Well, at least, I shall never know it.'

She might have continued for long in this fashion had not the voice of a crow directly overhead attracted her attention. Looking up to see what was the matter she beheld, in the dim light, a crow holding a fat frog in his claws, which he evidently intended for his supper.

The queen rose hastily from the seat, and striking the bird sharply on the claws with the fan which hung from her side, she forced him to drop the frog, which fell to the ground more dead than alive. The crow, furious at his disappointment, flew angrily away.

As soon as the frog had recovered her senses she hopped up to the queen, who was still sitting under the yew. Standing on her hind legs, and bowing low before her, she said gently:

'Beautiful lady, by what mischance do you come here? You are the only creature that I have seen do a kind deed since a fatal curiosity lured me to this place.'

'What sort of frog can you be that knows the language of mortals?' asked the queen in her turn. 'But if you do, tell me, I pray, if I alone am a captive, for hitherto I have beheld no one but the monsters of the lake.'

'Once upon a time they were men and women like yourself,' answered the frog, 'but having power in their hands, they used it for their own pleasure. Therefore fate has sent them here for a while to bear the punishment of their misdoings.'

'But you, friend frog, you are not one of these wicked people, I am sure?' asked the queen.

'I am a sort of fairy,' replied the frog. 'But, although I have certain magic gifts, I am not able to do all I wish. And if the Lion Fairy were to know of my presence in her kingdom she would hasten to kill me.'

'But if you are a fairy, how was it you were so nearly slain by the crow?' asked the queen, wrinkling her forehead.

'Because the secret of my power lies in my little cap made of rose leaves. I had laid it aside for the moment, when that horrible crow pounced upon me. Once it is on my head I fear nothing. But let me repeat; had it not been for you I could not have escaped death, and if I can do anything to help you or soften your hard fate, you have only to tell me.'

'Alas,' sighed the queen, 'I have been commanded by the Lion Fairy to make her a pasty out of the stings of bees and, as far as I can discover, there are none here; as how should there be, seeing there are no flowers for them to feed on? And, even if there were, how could I catch them?'

'Leave it to me,' said the frog, 'I will manage it for you.' And, uttering a strange noise, she struck the ground thrice with her foot. In an instant six thousand frogs appeared before her, one of them bearing a little cap.

'Cover yourselves with honey, and hop round by the bee-hives,' commanded the frog, putting on the cap which her friend was holding in her mouth. And turning to the queen, she added:

'The Lion Fairy keeps a store of bees in a secret place near the bottom of the ten thousand steps leading into the upper

world. Not that she wants them for herself, but they are sometimes useful to her in punishing her victims. However, this
time we will get the better of her.'

Just as she had finished speaking the six thousand frogs returned, looking so strange with bees sticking to every part of
them that, sad as she felt, the poor queen could not help laughing. The bees were all so stupefied with what they had eaten
that it was possible to draw their stings without hurting them.
So, with the help of her friend, the queen soon made ready her
pasty and carried it to the Lion Fairy.

'It is not bad,' said the giantess, gulping down large morsels,
in order to hide the surprise she felt. 'Well, you have escaped
this time, and I am glad to find I have a companion a little
more intelligent than the others I have tried. Now, you had
better go and build yourself a house.'

So the queen wandered away, and picking up a small axe
which lay near the door, she began with the help of her friend
the frog to cut down some cypress trees for the purpose. And
not content with that the six thousand frog servants were told
to help also, and it was not long before they had built the
prettiest little cabin in the world. They made a bed in one
corner of dried ferns which they fetched from the top of the
ten thousand steps. It looked soft and comfortable, and the
queen was very glad to lie down upon it, so tired was she with
all that had happened since the morning. Scarcely, however,
had she fallen asleep when the lake monsters began to make
the most horrible noises just outside, while a small dragon crept
in and terrified her so that she ran away, which was just what
the dragon wanted!

The poor queen crouched under a rock for the rest of the
night, and the next morning, when she woke from her troubled
dreams, she was cheered at seeing the frog watching by her.

'I hear we shall have to build you another palace,' said she. 'Well, this time we won't go so near the lake.'

And she smiled with her funny wide mouth, till the queen took heart, and they went together to find wood for the new cabin.

The tiny cabin was soon ready, and a fresh bed made of wild thyme, which smelt delicious. Neither the queen nor the frog said anything about it, but somehow, as always happens, the story came to the ears of the Lion Fairy, and she sent a raven to fetch the culprit.

'What gods or men are protecting you?' she asked, with a frown. 'This earth, dried up by a constant rain of sulphur and fire, produces nothing, yet I hear that your bed is made of sweet-smelling herbs. However, as you can get flowers for yourself, of course you can get them for me, and in an hour's time I must have in my room a nosegay of the rarest flowers. If not—! Now you can go.'

The poor queen returned to her house looking so sad that the frog, who was waiting for her, noticed it directly.

'What is the matter?' she asked, smiling.

'Oh, how can you laugh?' replied the queen. 'This time I have to bring to the Lion Fairy, in an hour, a posy of the rarest flowers, and where am I to find them? If I fail I know she will kill me.'

'Well, I must see if I can't help you,' answered the frog. 'The only person I have made friends with here is a bat. She is a good creature, and always does what I tell her, so I will just lend her my cap, and if she puts it on, and flies into the world, she will bring back all we want. I would go myself, only she will be quicker.'

Then the queen dried her eyes and waited patiently, and long before the hour had gone by the bat flew in with all the most beautiful and sweetest flowers that grew on the earth. The queen sprang up overjoyed at the sight, and hurried with them to the Lion Fairy, who was so astonished that for once she had nothing to say.

Now the smell and touch of the flowers had made the queen sick with longing for her home, and she told the frog that she would certainly die if she did not manage to escape somehow.

'Let me consult my cap,' said the frog; and taking it off she laid it in a box, and threw in after it a few sprigs of juniper, some capers, and two peas, which she carried under her right leg; she then shut down the lid of the box and murmured some words which the queen did not catch.

In a few moments a voice was heard speaking from the box.

'Fate, who rules us all,' said the voice, 'forbids your leaving this place till the time shall come when certain things are fulfilled. But, instead, a gift shall be given you, which will comfort you in all your troubles.'

And the voice spoke truly, for a few days afterward, when the frog peeped in at the door, she found the most beautiful baby in the world lying by the side of the queen.

'So the cap has kept its word,' cried the frog with delight. 'How soft its cheeks are and what tiny feet it has! What shall we call it?'

This was a very important point and needed much discussion. A thousand names were proposed and rejected for a thousand silly reasons. One was too long and one was too short. One was too harsh, another reminded the queen of somebody she did not like; but at length an idea flashed into the queen's head and she called out:

'I know! We will call her Muffette.'

'That is the very thing!' shouted the frog, jumping high into the air. And so it was settled.

The Princess Muffette was about six months old when the frog noticed that the queen had begun to grow sad again.

'Why do you have that look in your eyes?' she asked one day, when she had come in to play with the baby, who could now crawl. The frog was struck with the queen's sad face and lost no time in trying to find out the reason.

'I don't see what you have to complain of now; Muffette is quite well and quite happy, and even the Lion Fairy is kind to her when she sees her. What is it?'

'Oh, if her father could only see her!' cried the queen, clasping her hands. 'Or if I could only tell him all that has happened since we parted. But they will have brought him tidings of the broken carriage, and he will have thought me dead or devoured by wild beasts. And though he will mourn for me long—I know that well—yet in time they will persuade him to take a wife, and she will be young and fair, and he will forget me.'

And in all this the queen guessed truly, save that nine long years were to pass before he would consent to put another in her place.

The frog answered nothing at the time, but stopped her game and hopped away among the cypress trees. Here she sat and thought and thought, and the next morning she went back to the queen and said:

'I have come, madam, to make you an offer. Shall I go to the king instead of you, and tell him of your sufferings, and that he has the most charming baby in the world for his daughter? The way is long, and I travel slowly; but, sooner or later, I shall be sure to arrive. Only, are you not afraid to be left without my protection? Ponder the matter carefully; it is for you to decide.'

'Oh, it needs no pondering,' cried the queen joyfully, holding up her clasped hands, and making Muffette do likewise, in token of gratitude. But in order that he may know that you have come from me I will send him a letter.

And pricking her arm, she wrote a few words with her blood on the corner of her handkerchief. Then she gave it to the frog, and they bade each other farewell.

It took the frog a year and four days to mount the ten thousand steps that led to the upper world, but that was because she was still under the spell of a wicked fairy. By the time she reached the top, she was so tired that she had to remain for another year on the banks of a stream to rest, and also to arrange the procession with which she was to present herself before the King. For she knew far too well what was due to herself and her relations, to appear at court as if she was a mere nobody. At length, after many consultations with her cap, the affair was settled, and at the end of the second year after her parting with the queen they all set out.

First walked her bodyguard of grasshoppers, followed by her maids of honor, who were those tiny green frogs one sees in the fields, each one mounted on a snail and seated on a velvet saddle. Next came the water rats, dressed as pages, and lastly the frog herself, in a litter made of tortoiseshell and borne by eight toads. Here she could lie at her ease, with her cap on her head, for the litter was quite large and roomy, and could easily have held two eggs when the frog was not in it.

The journey lasted seven years, and all this time the queen suffered tortures of hope, though Muffette did her best to comfort her. Indeed, she would most likely have died had not the Lion Fairy taken a fancy that the child and her mother should go hunting with her in the upper world and, in spite of her sorrows, it was always a joy to the queen to see the sun again. As for little Muffette, by the time she was seven her arrows

seldom missed their mark. So, after all, the years of waiting
passed more quickly than the queen had dared to hope.

The frog was always careful to maintain her dignity and
nothing would have persuaded her to show her face in public
places, or even along the high road, where there was a chance
of meeting anyone. But sometimes, when the procession had to
cross a little stream, or go over a piece of marshy ground, orders
would be given for a halt; fine clothes were thrown off, bridles
were flung aside, and grasshoppers, water rats, even the frog
herself, spent a delightful hour or two playing in the mud.

But at length the end was in sight and the hardships were
forgotten in the vision of the towers of the king's palace. One
bright morning, the cavalcade entered the gates with all the
pomp and circumstance of a royal embassy. And surely no ambassador had ever created such a sensation! Doors and windows,
even the roofs of houses, were filled with people, whose cheers
reached the ears of the king. However, he had no time to attend
to such matters just then, for after nine years, he had at last
consented to the entreaties of his courtiers and was on the eve
of celebrating his second marriage.

The frog's heart beat high when her litter drew up before the
steps of the palace and, leaning forward, she beckoned to her
side one of the guards who were standing in his doorway.

'I wish to see his majesty,' said he.

'His majesty is engaged and can see no one,' answered the
soldier.

'His majesty will see me,' returned the frog, fixing her eye
upon him. And somehow the man found himself leading the
procession along the gallery into the Hall of Audience, where
the king sat surrounded by his nobles arranging the dresses
which everyone was to wear at his marriage ceremony.

All stared in surprise as the procession advanced, and still more when the frog gave one bound from the litter on to the floor, and with another landed on the arm of the chair of state.

'I am only just in time, sire,' began the frog, 'had I been a day later you would have broken your faith which you swore to the queen nine years ago.'

'Her remembrance will always be dear to me,' answered the king gently, though all present expected him to rebuke the frog severely for her impertinence. 'But know, Lady Frog, that a king can seldom do as he wishes, but must be bound by the desires of his subjects. For nine years I have resisted them; now I can do so no longer and have made choice of the fair young maiden playing at ball yonder.'

'You cannot wed her, however fair she may be, for the queen your wife is still alive and sends you this letter written in her own blood,' said the frog, holding out the handkerchief as she spoke. 'And, what is more, you have a daughter who is nearly nine years old, and more beautiful than all the other children in the world put together.'

The king turned pale when he heard these words, and his hand trembled so he could hardly read what the queen had written. Then he kissed the handkerchief and burst into tears, and it was some minutes before he could speak. When at length he found his voice he told his councillors that the writing was indeed that of the queen, and now that he had the joy of knowing she was alive he could, of course, proceed no further with his second marriage. This naturally displeased the ambassadors who had conducted the bride to court, and one of them inquired indignantly if he meant to put such an insult on the princess on the word of a mere frog.

'I am not a mere frog, and I will give you proof of it,' retorted the angry little creature. And putting on her cap, she cried:

'Fairies who are my friends, come hither!' And in a moment

a crowd of beautiful creatures, each one with a crown on her head, stood before her. Certainly none could have guessed that they were the snails, water rats and grasshoppers, from which she had chosen her retinue.

At a sign from the frog the fairies danced a ballet, with which everyone was so delighted that they begged to have it repeated; but now it was not youths and maidens who were dancing, but flowers. Then these again melted into fountains, whose waters interlaced and, rushing down the sides of the hall, poured out in a cascade down the steps and formed a river round the castle, with the most beautiful little boats upon it, all painted and gilded.

'Oh, let us go in them for a sail!' cried the princess, who had left her game of ball for a sight of these marvels. And, as she was bent upon it, the ambasadors, who had been charged never to lose sight of her, were obliged to go also, though they never entered a boat if they could help it.

But the moment they and the princess had seated themselves on the soft cushions, river and boats vanished, and the princess and the ambassadors vanished too. Instead, the snails and grasshoppers and water rats stood round the frog in their natural shapes.

'Perhaps,' said she, 'Your Majesty may now be convinced that I am a fairy and speak the truth. Therefore lose no time in setting in order the affairs of your kingdom and go in search of your wife. Here is a ring that will admit you into the presence of the queen, and will likewise allow you to address unharmed the Lion Fairy, though she is the most terrible crea-ture that ever existed.'

By this time the king had forgotten all about the princess, whom he had only chosen to please his people, and was as eager to depart on his journey as the frog was for him to go.

He made one of his ministers regent of the kingdom, and gave the frog everything her heart could desire; and with her ring on his finger he rode away to the outskirts of the forest. Here he dismounted, and bidding his horse go home, he pushed forward on foot.

Having nothing to guide him as to where he was likely to find the entrance of the Underworld, the king wandered hither and thither for a long while, till, one day, while he was resting under a tree, a voice spoke to him.

'Why do you give yourself so much trouble for nought, when you might know what you want to know for the asking? Alone you will never discover the path that leads to your wife.'

Much startled, the king looked about him. He could see nothing, and somehow, when he thought about it, the voice seemed as if it were part of himself. Suddenly his eyes fell on the ring, and he understood.

'Fool that I was!' cried he. 'How much precious time have I wasted? Dear ring, I beseech you, grant me a vision of my wife and my daughter!'

And even as he spoke there flashed past him a huge lioness, followed by a lady and a beautiful young maid mounted on fairy horses. Almost fainting with joy the king gazed after them, and then sank back trembling on the ground.

'Oh, lead me to them, lead me to them!' he exclaimed. And the ring, bidding him take courage, conducted him safely to the dismal place where his wife had lived for ten years.

Now the Lion Fairy knew beforehand of his expected presence in her dominions, and she ordered a palace of crystal to be built in the middle of the lake of quicksilver; and in order to make it more difficult of approach she let it float whither it would.

Immediately after their return from the chase, where the

king had seen them, she conveyed the queen and Muffette into the palace, and put them under the guard of the monsters of the lake, who one and all had fallen in love with the princess. They were horribly jealous, and ready to eat each other up for her sake, so they readily accepted the charge. Some stationed themselves round the floating palace, some sat by the door, while the smallest and lightest perched themselves on the roof.

Of course the king was quite ignorant of these arrangements and boldly entered the palace of the Lion Fairy, who was waiting for him, with her tail lashing furiously, for she still kept her lion's shape. With a roar that shook the walls she flung herself upon him; but he was on the watch, and a blow from his sword cut off the paw she had put forth to strike him dead. She fell back, and with his helmet still down and his shield up, he set his foot on her throat.

'Give me back the wife and the child you have stolen from me,' he said, 'or you shall not live another second!'

But the fairy answered: 'Look through the window at that lake and see if it is in my power to give them to you.'

The king looked, and through the crystal walls he beheld his wife and daughter floating on the quicksilver. At that sight the Lion Fairy and all her wickedness was forgotten. Flinging off his helmet, he shouted to them with all his might. The queen knew his voice, and she and Muffette ran to the window and held out their hands.

Then the king swore a solemn oath that he would never leave the spot without them if it should cost him his life; and he meant it, though at the moment he did not know what he was undertaking.

Three years passed by, and king was no nearer to obtaining his heart's desire. He had suffered every hardship that could be imagined—nettles had been his bed, wild fruits more bitter than gall his food, while his days had been spent in fighting the hideous monsters which kept him from the palace. He had not advanced one single step, nor gained one solitary advantage. Now he was almost in despair, and ready to defy everything and throw himself into the lake.

It was at this moment of his blackest misery that, one night, a dragon who had long watched him from the roof crept to his side.

'You thought that love would conquer all obstacles,' said he; 'well, you have found it hasn't! But if you will swear to me by your crown and scepter that you will give me a dinner of the food that I never grow tired of, whenever I choose to ask for it, I will enable you to reach your wife and daughter.'

Ah, how glad the king was to hear that! What oath would he not have taken so as to clasp his wife and child in his arms? Joyfully he swore whatever the dragon asked of him; then he jumped on its back, and in another instant would have been carried by the strong wings into the castle if the nearest monster had not happened to awake and hear the noise of talking and come to the shore to give battle.

The fight was long and hard, and when the king at last beat back his foes another struggle awaited him. At the entrance gigantic bats, owls, and crows set upon him from all sides; but the dragon had teeth and claws, while the queen broke off sharp bits of glass and stabbed and cut in her anxiety to help her husband.

At length the horrible creatures flew away; a sound like thunder was heard, the palace and the monsters vanished, while, at the same moment—no one knew how—the king found himself standing with his wife and daughter in the hall of his own home.

The dragon had disappeared with all the rest, and for some years no more was heard or thought of him.

Muffette grew every day more beautiful, and when she was fourteen the kings and emperors of the neighboring countries sent to ask her in marriage for themselves or their sons. For a long time the girl turned a deaf ear to all their prayers; but at length a young prince of rare gifts touched her heart, and though the king had left her free to choose the husband she would, he had secretly hoped that out of all the wooers this one might be his son-in-law. So they were betrothed that same day with great pomp, and then, with many tears, the prince set out for his father's court, bearing with him a portrait of Muffette.

The days passed slowly to Muffette, in spite of her brave efforts to occupy herself and not to sadden other people by her complaints. One morning she was playing on her harp in the queen's chamber when the king burst into the room and clasped his daughter in his arms with an energy that almost frightened her.

'Oh, my child! My dear child! Why were you ever born?' cried he, as soon as he could speak.

'Is the prince dead?' faltered Muffette, growing white and cold.

'No, no; but—oh, how can I tell you!' And he sank down on a pile of cushions while his wife and daughter knelt beside him.

At length he was able to tell his tale, and a terrible one it was! There had just arrived at court a huge giant, as ambassador from the dragon by whose help the king had rescued the queen and Muffette from the crystal palace.

The dragon had been very busy for many years past, and had quite forgotten the princess till the news of her betrothal had reached his ears. Then he remembered the bargain he had made with her father; and the more he heard of Muffette the more he felt sure she would make a delicious dish. So he had ordered the giant who was his servant to fetch her at once.

No words would paint the horror of both the queen and the princess as they listened to this dreadful doom. They rushed instantly to the hall, where the giant was awaiting them, and flinging themselves at his feet implored him to take the kingdom if he would, but to have pity on the princess. The giant looked at them kindly, for he was not at all hard-hearted, but said that he had no power to do anything, and that if the princess did not go with him quietly the dragon would come for her himself.

Several days went by, and the king and queen hardly ceased from entreating the aid of the giant, who by this time was weary of waiting.

'There is only one way of helping you,' he said at last, 'and that is to marry the princess to my nephew, who, besides being young and handsome, has been trained in magic, and will know how to keep her safe from the dragon.'

'Oh, thank you, thank you!' cried the parents, clasping his great hands to their breasts. 'You have indeed lifted a load from us. She shall have half the kingdom for her dowry.'

But Muffette stood up and thrust them aside.

'I will not buy my life with faithlessness,' she said proudly, 'and I will go with you this moment to the dragon's abode.'

And all her father's and mother's tears and prayers availed nothing to move her.

The next morning Muffette was put into a litter and, guarded by the giant and followed by the king and queen and the weeping maids of honor, they started for the foot of the mountain where the dragon had his castle. The way, though rough and stony, seemed all too short, and when they reached the spot appointed by the dragon, the giant ordered the men who bore the litter to stand still.

'It is time for you to bid farewell to your daughter,' said he, 'for I see the dragon coming to us.'

It was true; a cloud appeared to pass over the sun, for between them and it they could all discern dimly a huge body half a mile long approaching nearer and nearer.

At first the king could not believe that this was the small beast who had seemed so friendly on the shore of the lake of quicksilver; but then he knew very little of necromancy, and had never studied the art of expanding and contracting his body. But it was the dragon and nothing else, whose six wings were carrying him forward as fast as might be, considering his great weight and the length of his tail, which had fifty twists and a half.

He came quickly, yes; but the frog, mounted on a greyhound, and wearing her cap on her head, came quicker still. Entering a room where the prince was gazing at the portrait of his betrothed, she cried to him:

'What are you doing lingering here, when the life of the princess is nearing its last moment? In the courtyard you will find a green horse with three heads and twelve feet, and by its side a sword eighteen yards long. Hasten, lest you should be too late!'

The fight lasted all day, and the prince's strength was wellnigh spent, when the dragon, thinking that the victory was won, opened his jaws to give a roar of triumph. The prince saw his chance and, before his foe could shut his mouth again, had plunged his sword far down his adversary's throat. There was a desperate clutching of the claws to the earth, a slow flagging of the great wings, then the monster rolled over on his side and moved no more.

Muffette was saved.

After this they all went back to the palace. The marriage took place the following day, and Muffette and her husband lived happy forever after.

[From *Les Contes des Fées*, by Madame d'Aulnoy.]